SOLO ACT

For Sheri King Littlefield and Ann Stephens Poston.
I've cherished our friendship since kindergarten! Thanks for being like sisters to me.

Thanks to G Studios for dreaming up the Chosen Girls.
It's been fun bringing the dream to life!

The children's group of Zondervan

www.zonderkidz.com

Solo Act
Copyright © 2007 by G Studios, LLC

Requests for information should be addressed to:
Zonderkidz, Grand Rapids, Michigan 49530

Library of Congress Cataloging-in-Publication Data

Crouch, Cheryl, 1968-
    Solo act / by Cheryl Crouch.
        p. cm. -- (The Chosen Girls ; bk. 4)
    Summary: Mello wants to enjoy quiet time alone during a retreat at the
beach, but when The Chosen Girls are asked to play a concert and lead the
music at morning assemblies, her annoyance at being dragged into activities
prevents her from hearing the theme of the retreat--becoming a servant.
        ISBN-13: 978-0-310-71270-1 (softcover)
        ISBN-10: 0-310-71270-X (softcover)
        [1. Selfishness--Fiction. 2. Bands (Music)--Fiction. 3. Spiritual
retreats--Fiction. 4. Beaches--Fiction. 5. Christian life--Fiction.] I. Title.
PZ7.C8838Sol 2007
[Fic]--dc22
                                                    2006034383

Editor: Bruce Nuffer
Art direction and design: Sarah Molegraaf
Interior composition: Christine Orejuela-Winkelman

Printed in the United States of America

07 08 09 10 11 12 • 7 6 5 4 3 2 1

SOLO ACT

By Cheryl Crouch

zonder**kidz**

ZONDERVAN.com/
AUTHORTRACKER
follow your favorite authors

why can't harmony and trin
understand that i love them
but i can't always be Oh!

i need some time alone!

Melody

i just need some time—
free time.
a moment—just—to—be time.
time out with nothin' to prove.

Sunshine!

your <u>attitude</u> should be the same as that of
christ jesus: who, being in very nature god, did
not consider equality with god something to be
grasped, but made himself nothing, taking
the very nature of a servant, being
made in human likeness. —philippians 2:5–7

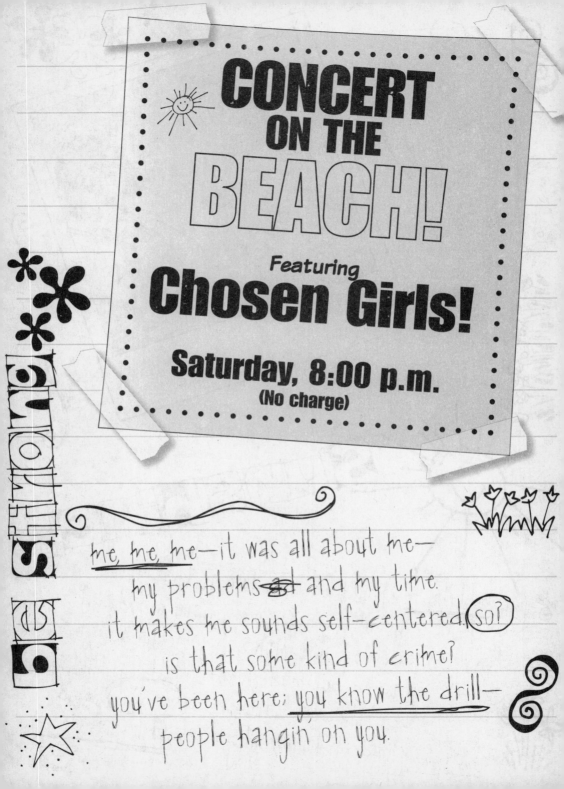

CONCERT ON THE BEACH!

Featuring

Chosen Girls!

Saturday, 8:00 p.m.
(No charge)

be strong

me, me, me—it was all about me—
my problems ~~at~~ and my time.
it makes me sounds self-centered. so?
is that some kind of crime?
you've been here; you know the drill—
people hangin' on you.

i love the sounds of moving water ... crashing waves, a splashing fountain, a pounding waterfall, dripping rain ... it's so (peaceful)

rock!

RAFFLE TICKET | 0015742
....
$1.00

what did ~~sh~~ candi hear me say? should i ask her? i really dont' want to hurt her. she is a really sweet kid, and we really connected on the beach when we talked about my brother and her sister. why did i have to make that awful comment? i can't seem to get anything right!!!!!

servanthood

sometimes i wish i was better at sports.
not like a varsity star or anything—just good
enough to be able to play a pickup game without
looking idiotic. i might have half a chance if i had a
little hand-eye coordination. but, no, i've got none.
zilch. zip. zero.

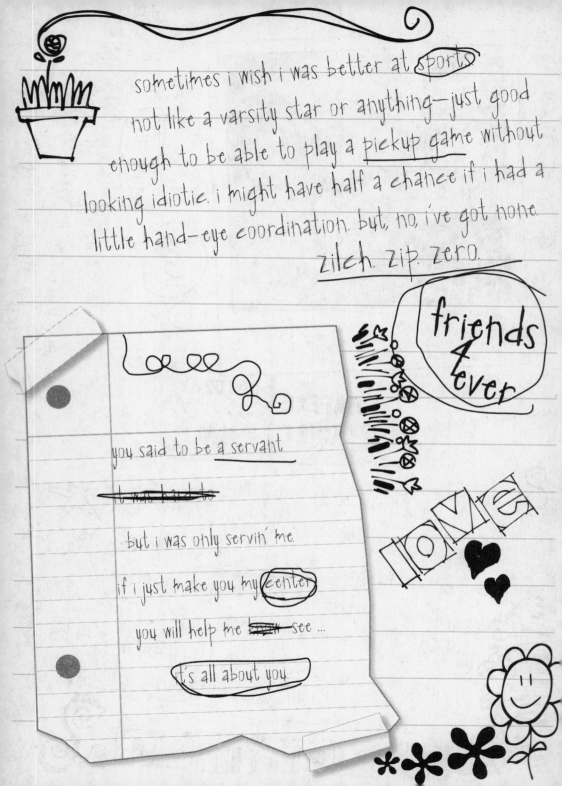

friends
4
ever

you said to be a servant

~~it was hard to~~

but i was only servin' me.

if i just make you my center

you will help me ~~even~~ see ...

it's all about you.

melody anne mcmann

- ✓ call trin
- ✓ pack
- ✓ finish song
- ✓ shop
- ✓ bake cookies!

ROCKIN

i'll fly away
amazing grace
standin' in the need of prayer
joyful, joyful we adore thee

dance

karson

karson and cole and hunter are coming on the retreat!!! when karson looks at me with his root-beer brown eyes, my stomach flips over. he is so gorgeous!

FUN *

[amott] is so funny. i like the way his brain works. he has been my neighbor for years, but he still surprised me with the great ideas he comes up with. i don't know what we would do without him!

breathe

what to pack
- ☑ fleece throw
- ☑ squishy pillow
- ☑ sleeping bag
- ☑ ~~two~~ three books!!!
- ☑ sunscreen
- ☑ swimsuits

MELODY

no time to rest; no place to breathe.
it had to bother you too.
but you choose to be nothing
instead of being selfish.
you became a servant
to teach me to be self-less.

YOUTH RETREAT
at Surf & Sand city
June 8-13

Come enjoy rollerblading,
mountain biking,
no way! horseback riding,
surfing,
kayaking, not doing that!
horseshoes,
tetherball,
volleyball and **more**! relax!!!

chapter • 1

...

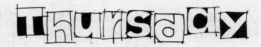

My life used to be simple. All I needed: a good book and my fluffy fleece blanket.

Then everything changed with the Trinvasion. Since Trin Adams moved here and took over our lives, my best friend Harmony and I have never been the same.

Sure, I'm glad Trin talked us into being a rock band. I'm a real drummer now. But I don't like being out front, even though I can do it. Thankfully, I won't have to worry about that for a while.

Now summer's here, school's over, and my only scheduled gig is going to Surf & Sand City, where Harmony and I spend a week every year — huge cliffs overlooking the ocean, tons of cute boys, and time to read and do a whole bunch of nothing.

But best of all, no band, no work, and no Trin . . .

• • •

I had just rolled into my softest fleece throw and shuffled to my bookshelf to choose a book when my cell phone rang "La Bamba."

"Harmony?"

"Hello, Mello!" Harmony's voice blasted out at me. "Are you packed?"

"Packing."

"I knew it. Are you ready for some serious fun-o-rama?"

"I'm ready for some rest-o-rama, Harmony—picking out a novel as we speak."

I could practically hear her rolling her eyes.

"You've got to be the only teenager in Southern California who thinks a retreat at Surf & Sand City is about resting," she accused.

"You can do whatever you want," I answered. "You'll know where to find me."

"On your favorite cliff, reading a book," she said in her most disgusted voice.

I closed my eyes and pictured it. I could almost smell the ocean and feel the breeze. "Definitely."

"I can't believe we leave tomorrow. One o'clock, just like last year?"

"Definitely."

"And you signed us up to room together, right?"

"Definitely."

"Hasta mañana!"

I punched the End button on my phone. Before I even put it down, it rang again. But it wasn't "La Bamba."

"Hello?"

"May I please speak to Mello McMann?"

"This is she," I answered.

"Mello, this is David Karuthers. You know that I'm coordinating this year's retreat. Today I'm pulling together last-minute details at the office. Are you coming to choir practice tonight?" he asked in his bouncy voice.

"Yes," I answered, trying to figure out what choir had to do with anything.

"Do you think your friend Harmony could come with you? And maybe you could come early? I'd like to speak to the two of you about the trip."

I paused before I answered. Was this about last year's retreat? The speaker's shoes hot-glued to the ceiling? Or the toothpaste on the pillows? Or maybe the water-balloon launcher?

If so, he needed to talk to Harmony, not me. Maybe it wasn't the best idea to invite her to join my youth group on this trip every year.

I said, "I think so. I'll call Harmony."

"Great. Meet me at the youth center at six thirty."

•••

"If I was going to get in trouble for that stuff, don't you think it would have happened last year?" Harmony whispered as we walked up the church sidewalk.

I shrugged. "Maybe they found out something new. Maybe someone just now complained. How should I know?"

"So why do you have to be here? All you did last year was read."

I threw an arm around Harmony's shoulder. "I guess I'm guilty by association," I said with a groan.

We found Mr. Karuthers inside the youth center. He didn't look mad at all. He smiled real wide, bounced over to some chairs, and pulled three of them into a triangle.

"Here, girls, have a seat," he said. "Thanks for coming."

I looked at Harmony, and she raised her eyebrows. So far, so good.

"Mello, Harmony, I want this retreat to be a special time for everyone who attends. I know it's a good time to relax, but I think it should be more than that."

Harmony shot me a look. I felt like saying, "I don't think he's talking about pranks and water-balloon fights."

"Last night I went down the list of students who will be attending," he continued. "When I got to your names, I knew I had the answer I've been looking for!"

My heart started beating out a warning. I didn't want to be anyone's answer to anything. I wanted to hide on my cliff and read.

He smiled at us and asked, "How would the Chosen Girls like to do an outreach concert on the beach Saturday night?"

"Cool frijoles!" Harmony said, probably as much from relief about not being in trouble as from excitement about the concert.

I tried to process. One concert wouldn't be such a big deal. I would only lose one evening of downtime. But I would have to bring my drums. And Trin.

It wasn't what I had planned on.

Mr. Karuthers talked on and on about how all the campers could pass out flyers Friday. Loads of people would come. He said the concert would be a great opportunity for people to hear the positive message our band loved to share.

I started simmering inside. *I don't care if those people hear our message, Mr. Karuthers. I want to read my book, not do a concert.*

But I smiled and said, "Definitely, Mr. Karuthers. We'll check with Trin, but I'm sure she'll say yes. Can our sound-man come too?"

•••

Lamont agreed immediately, offering to help with more than sound. He'd always wanted to go to Surf & Sand City. And Trin definitely said yes. Actually, she screamed, "Ohwow! Yes! Sweet! I can't wait! What should I pack?"

I knew Trin had been feeling left out since Harmony and I had planned to go without her. I finished packing and spent the rest of the night chatting online.

Trin: *ohwow — it's right on the beach?*

Harmony: *sí. muy bonita. bring sunscreen.*

Trin: *sand volleyball?*

Me: *n surfing lessons, horses, mountain biking*

Harmony: *LOL! like mello ever did any of that b4!!! but u will luv it, trin — just wait til u c the cabins. way cute*

Trin: *i can't wait. i just have 2 learn 2 surf!*

Lamont: *i haven't been on a board in months*

Me: *thx for the warning — we'll stay out of ur way*

Trin: *how many pairs of shoes r u bringing?*

Me: *2*

Lamont: *what does THAT matter?*

Harmony: *be quiet, Lamont. i packed 5*

Trin: *i think i can make it with 8*

Lamont: *we're only there a week. why do u need 8 pairs of shoes?*

Trin: *didn't some1 tell u 2 b quiet?*

I could see Harmony was psyched about Trin's going. Now she'd have someone to hang with. I should have been happy for her, since I just wanted to kick back. But instead I felt irritated.

•••

Friday morning we met early at the shed behind my house. Harmony and I had used the shed as a playhouse for years, but now it serves as a studio. We needed to run through the songs and make sure we were all cool with the plan. Lamont joined us, since he lives right next door.

I did some rolls on the snare to warm up. Harmony got out her bass, and Trin started tuning her electric. I asked what song we should start with.

Trin looked past me, smiled her hugest smile, and said, "I can just imagine pounding to the edge of a cliff on the back of a black stallion, overlooking the Pacific Ocean—"

"Just don't run over Mello. She'll be sitting on that cliff, reading," Harmony said.

I shook my head. "If we don't get started, I'll never get to chill. We'll be practicing the whole time."

"Should I bring the camera?" Lamont asked. "I can tape the concert."

"A concert on the beach!" Harmony said. "It might be our biggest one yet. Sí, tape it!"

"But in order to do a concert, we'll have to know what song we're opening with," I reminded them. "Which brings us back to why we're here this—"

"Are we changing to superhero suits halfway through?" Harmony interrupted.

"Wait! I forgot to pack mine!" Trin said, already walking across the room. "And my white boots. Ohwow, I better go right now." She packed her guitar into the case. "And I forgot bracelets! I so am not good with last-minute packing."

"You definitely should do the super suits," Lamont said. "That's your trademark. It's what makes the Chosen Girls stand out. Either super suits or chicken suits."

Harmony whirled to face him. "The chicken disaster is over. Do not mention the chicken suits, the chicken concert, or the chicken jingle unless you want me to practice my newest karate move on you."

Lamont shut his mouth, but he started humming the tune for *Chik'n Quik / Chicken on a stick / It's so yummy for your tummy / Everybody loves Chik'n Quik.*

Harmony put her guitar on the couch and raised her arms to fighting position.

"You didn't say I couldn't hum!" Lamont cried, crossing his arms in front of his face in self-defense.

"What about our practice?" I asked Trin. "We didn't even run through one song."

"We'll have to do it when we get there," she said as she ran out the door. "See you at one!"

Harmony put her arms down, and Lamont sighed in mock relief. She grabbed her bass, put it in the case, and fastened the latches. "Know what? I forgot my new bracelets too!" she said. "And I think I should take my purple flip-flops." She moved toward the door.

"Harmony," I whined. "I don't want to spend the whole time we're there practicing for the concert."

She looked back at me. "Don't worry, Mello. We'll be fine," she said. Then she left too.

I looked at Lamont. "Please don't tell me you need to pack bracelets or flip-flops," I begged him.

He shrugged. "Nope. But I do need to get my camera and the charger and—"

"Fine!" I said. "Just go."

He walked toward the door and said, "Mello, the concert will be great. The Chosen Girls can do this with their eyes closed. What's wrong with you?"

I shook my head. I did know one thing—now that the Chosen Girls were officially involved, this retreat would be anything but downtime.

...

chapter 2

Friday Afternoon

We'd been on the road only five minutes when Harmony, Trin, and Lamont started singing "Ninety-nine Bottles of Coke on the Wall" at the top of their lungs. The whole bus joined in, but not loud enough to drown out Lamont, who didn't hit one right note. I thought, *There's more than one reason you don't sing in the band.*

I pulled out my book and tried to get lost in the story.

"Ninety-two bottles of Coke. Take one down, pass it around. Ninety-one bottles of Coke on the wall."

"Hey! Look at that red convertible!"

"Where?"

"Out the left window, one lane over."

"Wow! A brand-new Mercedes."

"What verse were we on?"

"I don't remember. Let's start over."

"Ninety-nine bottles of Coke on the wall. Ninety-nine bottles of Coke ..."

I gritted my teeth and read the first sentence for the fourth time. They made it to eighty-two bottles before Trin yelled, "Ohwow! Look at all those palm trees with the ocean behind them."

"Yeah. Highway 1 is the coolest highway in California."

"Look at those waves crashing."

"Serious surfing ahead, dudes."

"Hey, what verse were we on?"

"I don't remember. Let's start over."

"Ninety-nine bottles of Coke on the wall, ninety-nine bottles of Coke ..."

"We're here!" Harmony yelled.

"Surf & Sand City," Lamont read from the tall wooden sign that spanned the entryway. The sign looked rustic — the on-purpose kind of rustic, where something is brand-spanking-new but they want it to look like it's always been there. That's how everything looks at Surf & Sand City.

"What should we do first?" Trin asked as the bus pulled into the perfectly manicured grounds.

I rolled my eyes. "How about put our stuff in the cabins?" I didn't mean for it to sound snotty, but all that Coke on the wall had put me over the edge.

She looked hurt. "Well, yeah. I meant after that."

We made plans to meet Lamont later. Then we hauled our bags to our cabin: a tiny cedar-shake building with a door, four windows, four twin beds, and a desk.

"Ohwow!" Trin gushed, plopping her bright pink sleeping bag onto a bed. "It's way fabulous. Our own little cottage!"

"And listen," Harmony told her, throwing her suitcase on a different bed. "When it's quiet, you can hear the waves."

I looked at the two of them. "Not that we ever expect it to be quiet. But it's a nice thought."

"Let's hit the beach. I want to hear the ocean up close and feel the spray on my face," Harmony said as she opened her suitcase and pulled out her swimsuit.

We changed quickly, threw on our cover-ups, and went to find Lamont's cabin.

"Forty-three," Trin said, reading the small numbers by the window. "This is it."

Harmony banged on the door. "What's taking so long?" she yelled. "You should be embarrassed that three girls can get ready faster than you."

The door swung open, and I caught my breath. Karson — the beyond-cute bass player for KCH — stood there smiling his lopsided grin. "Sorry," he said. "Didn't know we were invited."

Harmony stammered, "So-so-sorry. We thought Lamont was in forty-three."

Cole, who is Harmony's forever crush, stepped to the door beside Karson. "Yeah. He's in here. Want me to send him out?"

"Please," Trin answered. "We're ready for the ocean."

Cole yelled over his shoulder, "Hey, your girlfriends are here. We're gonna start callin' you Lucky Lamont."

Lamont came to the doorway and playfully pushed Cole and Karson aside. Then he struck a bodybuilder pose and flashed us a big smile. His long, bony arms made me giggle. "I'm ready, women," he said. He switched and flexed his invisible muscles on the other side. "As you can see, it was worth the wait."

The ocean made up for the miserable bus ride. I felt the tension easing out of my body as I floated on my back up and down on the waves. I felt the rhythm, heard the crashing, and smelled the air, tasting salt when I licked my lips. It felt like we'd just gotten in the water when Harmony said, "OK, amigas. Everybody refreshed?"

Trin said, "Yeah, we better practice if we're gonna be done in time for that opening mixer you told me about."

"Mixer?" Lamont asked as we walked through the waves to the sandy beach.

Harmony grabbed a towel and started drying off. "The retreat always kicks off with crazy games where you get to know everybody, since people come from all over Southern Cal." She winked at me and Trin. "More cute boys than you can shake a Frisbee at."

I looked back at the ocean, mad about practice. I growled inside all the way to the cabin, while we changed clothes, and then as we carried our instruments into the auditorium.

We made it through two songs and had started on the third when Mr. Karuthers burst in. His face looked all red and blotchy.

I asked, "What's wrong?"

"One of the other leaders had to rush Mrs. Deerheart to the hospital. She's gone into early labor."

Trin freaked. "Ohwow. How far along was she? Will the baby be OK? What can we do?" Then she asked, "Uh, who is Mrs. Deerheart anyway?"

Mr. Karuthers paused, like he had to think about which question to answer first. "Um, she and the baby will be fine, but she obviously won't be back to the retreat. And she was going to lead our music during the morning assemblies."

I closed my eyes. *Here it comes.*

"I know leading music is a whole different ball game from doing concerts, but I thought since your band is here and you have your instruments, maybe you'd like to give it a try. What do you think, Mello?"

I guess he looked at me because he knows me. I looked at Trin and Harmony.

"Every morning?" Harmony asked.

Trin said, "Ohwow. That's, like, a really big deal. Do you think we're ready for that?"

I expected them to jump up and down. They usually go crazy for a chance to be up front. Because of them, we'd already done everything *but* lead music. Why did they suddenly sound nervous?

Lamont asked, "Have any of you ever done this before?"

We all shook our heads. Lamont looked down, like he thought the task was too big.

"You'd really be helping me out. I'm kinda stuck," Mr. Karuthers said. He looked at each of us. "I know you came expecting to relax. So if you do this, we'll cover the retreat cost for all of you. I might even be able to rustle up some spending money."

Harmony's face broke into a smile. "*Muy bueno!*" she yelled. "I say sī."

"Oh, happy day!" Lamont agreed, looking up. "We can handle this."

Trin nodded. "We know the songs," she said. "I mean, we sing them at youth group, right? How hard can it be?"

They all looked at me. I sighed and tried to fight the tears as I said good-bye to my cliff and my book. I forced my face into a cheesy, fake smile. "Sure, Mr. Karuthers. We'll do it."

left, Trin said, "OK, the concert is *so* on the back

're leading music in the morning! Any ideas?"

ony said, "Let's try a classic — something everyone

ow. Like a revved-up version of 'Amazing Grace.'"

arted on the drums. Harmony and Trin joined in on

r guitars.

"What is that?" Trin asked, stopping halfway through and staring at Harmony.

Harmony played another twang on her bass. "I thought we could give it a country-and-western feel."

"That explains it," Trin said. "I'm thinking punk rock."

"Scary combo," Lamont commented. "Maybe you should play it straight once, before you get too crazy."

I nodded in agreement. "Good idea. 'Amazing Grace.' Basic version." I tapped the beats and started on snare. Trin started singing, and I sang harmony. We had to stop a few times to remember the words of the verses.

"Do you have these songs written down anywhere?" Trin asked me.

"No," I answered (a little louder than I meant to). "Why should I? I thought this was going to be a retreat. I thought I would be sitting on a cliff reading a book. I didn't know I was going to end up practically running the whole thing!"

Everyone froze and stared at me.

Harmony said, "Mello, go get Mr. Karuthers. Tell him we aren't ready for this. Tell him you need a break. He can find someone else."

Great. Now my best friend thought I couldn't handle it.

"I'm not calling him back," I snapped. "I gave my word. So we're going to lead music, and we're going to do a good job."

But that doesn't mean I have to be happy about it, I thoug

Trin and Mello looked at each other. Lamont looked at the ceiling.

"So ... country or punk?" Harmony finally asked.

"Country," Trin answered. "And we better stick to the first verse."

"I know where some song sheets are." The voice came from the back of the auditorium. I saw a chunky girl, maybe twelve years old, with super-curly, short red hair and freckles that showed all the way across the building.

"Song sheets?" I asked.

She walked toward us. "You know, papers with all the words to all the songs. That would help, right?"

"Oh, happy day!" Lamont said. "What is your name, angel of mercy?"

She laughed. "I'm Candi. My parents are the caretakers for Surf & Sand City." She disappeared behind a huge wooden podium and came out on the other side waving a stack of papers. "I love the drums," she said, handing the stack to me.

"Candi, these are perfect!" I told her, shuffling through the sheets. "Listen: 'I Will Sing of the Mercies of the Lord Forever,' 'Standin' in the Need of Prayer,' 'I Have Decided' ... all the classics."

She smiled at me like no one else was in the room. Then she crossed her legs and sat down—right next to my drum set.

I looked at Harmony. She shrugged. "So you live here, Candi? How cool is that?"

Candi didn't take her eyes off my face. She answered, "Yeah. How long have you played the drums?"

I looked into her light blue eyes. "Since I was seven," I answered. She looked a little sad. I added, "But lots of people start when they're older," and she smiled again.

d her throat. "Well, let's get started again, now

ot words. We need … what? Four or five songs?"

h service," Harmony added.

t shook his head. "So long, mixer."

. We're gonna be practicing every spare minute," Trin

ed.

rolled my eyes. "So long, retreat."

• • •

The sun had gone down by the time we left the auditorium. Candi followed me all the way to the cabin. "Well, I guess you better get back now," I told her. "I'm sure your parents are worried."

"Nah," she answered, standing on the porch.

I shut the door halfway. "See you in the morning," I said, and shut it the rest of the way.

"Poor kid," Trin said. "She must not get enough attention."

Harmony giggled. "Mello has a fan!"

"Looks like she'll get plenty of opportunity to hear me play, doesn't it?" I griped. I grabbed my pj's and toothbrush and slammed out of the cabin. I was stomping along the dark path to the bathhouse when I heard, "Hi, Mello."

I screamed and jumped about two feet in the air.

"Sorry," Candi said.

I started walking again, and she followed me, talking the whole time.

"Didn't mean to scare you. I can't wait to listen to your band in the morning. You sound great. You're a really good drummer."

I went in, wet my toothbrush, and put toothpaste on it.

"I've always wanted to play the drums. They're the coolest instruments ever. Mom makes me take piano, but I can't stand it."

I finished brushing, spit, and said, "It must be fun to live at Surf & Sand City." I wished she'd go away while I rinsed out my mouth.

"This is a pretty fun place to live, I guess. I get to surf and ride horses and Rollerblade and mountain bike all I want. But I wish I had my own drums."

I smiled at her before I slipped into a stall to change.

"I'm going to watch you play all week. Maybe I'll learn something just from watching. 'Cause you're the best. I can tell."

I gritted my teeth. She followed me back to the cabin.

"I asked for drums for Christmas this year. Even if I get them, I bet I'll never be as good as you. I'm glad you'll be playing every morning. And practicing all the time. That is what Trin said, isn't it? You'll be practicing *all the time*, right?"

I forced one more smile and said, "Definitely. All the time," before I shut the door in her face. Ignoring Harmony and Trin, I jumped into bed, facing the wall. When the first tear slid down my face, I stuck my tongue out and caught it.

Salty, just like the ocean.

chapter • 3

...

Saturday Morning

"Who made up the schedule for this retreat?" Trin complained, sliding her tray along the metal counter in the dining
hall. "Breakfast at seven thirty in the *morning*!"

I pushed my tray along behind her and said, "Yeah, crazy,
isn't it? Serving breakfast in the *morning*." I smiled at the
woman behind the counter and said, "Yes, please." She
plopped a blob of bright yellow scrambled eggs onto our
plates. Trin stared at the blobs with water oozing around
the edges.

"Instant eggs," Harmony whispered. She smiled at the
woman and said, "No, thank you."

I grabbed one of the oatmeal packets.

"So who's going to show for an eight thirty session?" Trin
asked, picking up a glass and filling it with orange juice.

"Actually, everyone," I answered, grabbing an apple juice.
"It's required."

"Sí, there should be about three hundred people," Harmony added. "But it doesn't mean they want to be there."

We chose a table and quickly said grace.

"Mind if these guys join us?" Lamont asked. I looked up, and there he stood with Karson, Cole, and Hunter. Each one had a tray loaded with about three days' worth of food.

Harmony said, "We've got plenty of room."

Karson grinned at me as he put his tray down. I looked into his root-beer brown eyes, and my stomach flipped over. I knew I couldn't take another bite. "So, you ready to surf? Rollerblade?" he asked. "What are you into?"

I couldn't say, "reading." How lame would that sound? So I said, "Sure. All of it."

Harmony snorted. Then she turned to Cole and asked, "So did Lamont tell you we're doing music for morning assemblies this week?"

Cole nodded. "Yeah. Tough break."

Harmony and I looked at each other. What did that mean?

Trin said, "Eat fast, Lamont. We need to get over and check sound."

"Ready," he answered.

I looked at his tray. Empty. Not a crumb left.

"How can you eat that fast? Do you just inhale and it's gone?" I asked.

"Pretty much. Let's go," he answered.

• • •

Harmony was right about morning assembly. Three hundred cranky, been-up-most-of-the-night teenagers slunk in, huddled into seats, crossed their arms, and scowled at us.

They made it pretty tough to smile while we played the preliminary music.

Mr. Karuthers walked to the podium. "Good morning, everyone!" he yelled into the mike. "I am so excited about our music for morning assemblies this week."

The back door opened, and I groaned. Makayla and the Snob Mob shuffled in, looking for seats.

I caught Harmony's eye and jerked my head toward the back row of seats.

"They never come to retreat!" Harmony whispered in surprise.

I raised my eyebrows. "Guess there's a first for everything."

Trin mumbled, "As if dealing with them at school isn't bad enough. I thought this was called summer *break*. When do we get a break from *them*?"

"So put your hands together," Mr. Karuthers said, "and welcome the Chosen Girls!"

I heard one person clapping energetically. Candi. In the front row. Maybe ten other people made a weak attempt at applause — and four of those were Lamont and KCH.

Makayla's head jerked up when he said "Chosen Girls." I could see her laughing already, pointing at us.

"We're going to start with a classic," Trin said into the mike. She sounded nervous. "We know you know it, so please sing with us." We launched into "Amazing Grace," country-style.

A few people sang. I could hear Candi's voice above the rest. She actually sounded decent, and I almost forgave her for driving me insane the night before. Halfway through the chorus, Makayla yelled, "Yee-haw!" and everybody laughed.

The other songs didn't go much better. I watched the kids in the back whispering, playing with cell phones, and wandering in and out.

Doing a concert—my scariest thing—suddenly seemed as easy as taking a raspberry-scented bubble bath. At a concert, it didn't matter if people sang along, but they did anyway. Now, when singing along was the whole point, no one even bothered to *listen*.

We finally wrapped it up and went to our seats on the fourth row. Candi motioned frantically for me to move up by her.

"Go," Harmony whispered. "She's our only supporter. You have to keep her happy."

When Mr. Karuthers had us stand for prayer, I moved up. Candi rewarded me with a huge smile and a hug.

After prayer, an older guy with a buzz cut and wearing a T-shirt and denim shorts jogged to the podium and said, "I can't stand annoying questions. You know, like, 'Are you looking forward to summer break?' Please! How obvious is that? There isn't a person on the planet who doesn't count the seconds till summer break. Or the opposite extreme—'What do you want to *be* when you grow up?' My brain starts hurting when I think of all the possible answers!"

Candi giggled beside me, and I smiled.

The speaker said, "Try this answer to that last one: 'I'd really like to be a servant.' That will stop them in their tracks. Because serving ... That's not a hot job in our culture. Becoming CEO of a Fortune 500 company or a brain surgeon or a trial lawyer—that's what they want to hear. Not a lot of people scan the want ads, saying, 'I just want to be a servant.'

"Please turn to Philippians 2:5 – 7."

I found it in my Bible and held it out so Candi could read along as the speaker recited the passage:

> *Your attitude should be the same as that of*
> *Christ Jesus: Who, being in very nature God, did*

not consider equality with God something to be grasped, but made himself nothing, taking the very nature of a servant, being made in human likeness.

"So people don't often have servanthood as a goal," he continued. "But the Bible says we should. And Jesus—God himself—is our example. Of course I'm not really talking about career goals. I'm talking about lifestyle.

"What does it mean to be a servant? Think of a waiter, or server, at a restaurant. What makes a good server? Would he come up and say, 'Welcome to Bob's Burger Barn. Go in the kitchen and get me a cheeseburger. I'm starving! And get me a Diet Coke while you're at it'? Then would he look at you and say, 'What are you sitting around for? Pull out a chair for me! My feet are tired and my back hurts'? No! Because a server can't think of himself. A server has to think of others."

Good! I thought. *I hope Trin and Harmony are listening. All they care about is being up front and getting attention. That's the total opposite of servanthood. If they had been thinking about* me *at all, this retreat would be more of a retreat.*

Okay, so I'm the one who said we'd lead music. But I only said yes because it's what they wanted. At least someone *in the band thinks of others.*

My cell phone vibrated. I pulled it out and found a text message from Trin:

Tough crowd.

So they weren't listening. Probably too busy whispering about the music. I punched in my reply:

Me: *definitely*

Harmony: *we reeked*

Me: *definitely*
Trin: *no more country music*
Me: *definitely*
Harmony: *can u say anything but* definitely?
Me: *definitely*

After assembly, Candi followed us down a shady path that wove between flowerbeds. We headed in the general direction of our cabin at the other end of Surf & Sand City. "You sounded great this morning!" Candi bubbled.

I rolled my eyes. "Please. We were dying a slow, painful death up there. Very slow and painful—it's going to last all week!"

"I think we flopped because Harmony picked too many real songs," Trin complained. "It's camp, right? We're supposed to do fun songs. 'Oil in My Lamp' and 'Deep and Wide' stuff. Maybe then people would sing."

I shuddered, picturing us onstage leading cheesy hand motions.

"Why didn't you say that last night at practice?" Harmony asked Trin. "Besides, if we want our time to count as worship, we need to sing something besides fluffy music. And just in case you forgot, *I'm* the band manager."

Trin's jaw dropped. "Do *not* go there, Harmony. I am so aware that I *only* play electric and sing lead."

Lamont walked up behind us. "Hey," he said, "how many lead singers does it take to change a lightbulb?" Then he held up his pointer finger and said, "Only one. She holds the lightbulb, and the world revolves around her."

Harmony and I cracked up, but not Trin. "I wouldn't think a drummer would want to get started on musician jokes," she said, looking right at me.

"Why?" I asked.

She said, "You asked for it. What does it mean when the drummer drools out both sides of her mouth?"

"Huh?" Lamont asked, kicking a pebble along as we walked.

"The stage is level," Trin answered with a smirk.

Candi looked up at me. "I don't get it."

I glared at Trin and explained, "It means drummers are so stupid they can't even swallow."

Candi glared at Trin too.

"Ouch," Harmony said, plucking a leaf off a bush next to the path. "I'm glad I play bass."

"Know why bands have bass players?" Trin continued.

"Why?" Lamont asked.

Trin giggled and answered, "To translate for the drummer."

"OK," Harmony interrupted with a shake of her head. "Let's quit beating ourselves up. There are enough other people ready to do that. Besides, I don't think it's entirely our fault. What about the people in assembly? Can you believe how rude they acted during the music?"

"For reals!" Trin agreed. "Did they really have to go in and out that many times? Aren't they old enough to sit still?"

Lamont paused as the dining hall came into view. "Do you think they serve snacks between meals?"

"Lamont!" I said. "You just ate enough breakfast to feed a small country for a week. How can you be hungry already?"

"And they all just kept talking!" Harmony continued, ignoring Lamont and me. "They didn't even seem to notice we were onstage."

"The cell phones drive me crazy," I said. "Why can't people leave them alone for fifteen minutes?"

"Great job, Chosen Girls!" Mr. Karuthers boomed, bouncing out of the dining hall. "Best music we've ever had in morning assembly. Sure appreciate you helping me out."

I smiled at him. "Thanks! We're enjoying it."

Harmony looked at me in shock.

"I do have one request, though," Mr. Karuthers added. "Since you're in leadership this year, I'd like you to be examples. So could you cut out the whispering and messing with your cell phones while the speaker is speaking? Thanks," he said and bounded away.

I put my hand over the cell phone in my pocket. "I guess we're as bad as everyone else," I mumbled.

"Thanks, Mr. Karuthers!" Harmony crooned the moment he disappeared. "We're enjoying leading music." She pointed at me and asked, "What was that, liar?"

"Humph! It's called being polite," I answered.

"Man," Lamont said, shaking his head. "You women are cold-blooded. I'm out of here." He loped off toward the tetherball poles.

"He's right. *Por favor,* let's forget about music for a while, or we're going to kill each other. Let's do something fun," Harmony begged. "We've got a little time before we have to practice again."

Trin lit up. "Let's kayak."

I groaned. "But then we have to paddle. And be coordinated. I don't want to work; I want to relax."

"Kayaking isn't work," Trin said with a laugh. "It's perfect for you. It's quiet and peaceful, and it's out in nature. Come on!" She and Harmony headed for the boat dock.

I watched them go. Maybe I could grab my book or take a nap.

Candi tugged my elbow. "Wanna go to your cabin and talk?"

A morning with Candi fawning over me would be worse than kayaking. I started after Trin and Harmony. "Sorry. I guess I better go with them," I told her.

Harmony turned around. "Candi, I bet you've paddled a lot, haven't you?"

Candi nodded, her red curls bobbing.

"Why don't you come with us?" Trin asked. "You can share a kayak with Mello."

chapter • 4

...

Saturday Morning

We passed the tetherball poles on our way to the docks and saw Lamont playing Cole. When we walked by, Cole grunted and whacked the tetherball soundly. The rope sang as it twisted around the pole. Lamont jumped and missed, and the game ended with the ball at the very top. Cole held his fists above his head in victory and yelled, "Yes!"

"Come kayak with us," Harmony called.

Lamont shook his head. "I'd rather lose another game than listen to you women peck each other to death."

"We're not going to talk about music," Trin said. "Promise."

Harmony grinned at Cole. "Besides, Lamont, who said I was talking to you?"

Cole smiled at her. He chucked Lamont on the shoulder and said, "Come on."

So they followed us to the kayaks.

The banana-shaped boats were tucked between two docks inside a small bay. On either side, sandy cliffs reached long arms into the ocean. "Dad calls this Candi's Cove," Candi whispered as we got closer. In the middle, the dark brown beams of the docks jutted out thirty feet or so, floating on gentle blue-green waves.

"Getting in and out is the hardest part," Candi explained as she handed us each a life jacket and a paddle from the supply shack. We put the life vests on and followed her down the dock, where she used her paddle to pull a kayak closer. "See, the seat straps are buckled around these wires." She tugged on a heavy wire that ran between the docks. The kayaks attached to it bobbed up and down.

As she pulled a kayak alongside the dock, she handed me her paddle. "Will you hold this for me while I get in?" she asked. Then she stepped off the dock and into the kayak as easily as stepping off a front porch onto the sidewalk. Except that the "porch" was three feet high, and the "sidewalk" wiggled like Jell-O on a spoon. She sat in the backseat and reached for her paddle.

I looked at the kayak bobbing below me in the water, with Candi just waiting to talk my ear off. Such a small boat for two of us. "Really, I think I'll hang here on the dock . . . ," I began.

"Get in!" Trin yelled. "If you don't hurry, it will be time for lunch."

I got in my seat without falling into the ocean. Candi unclipped our kayak from the wire, and we fastened our seat straps. I tried to use my paddle to back us away from the dock. Candi kept correcting me: "Use the right side — no, the left." "Dip deeper." "Don't push so hard."

I was already sick of the trip, and we hadn't gone five feet.

The boys got in last and immediately declared a race. They shot ahead like Olympic contestants.

"Let them go," I said.

"No way!" Candi answered. "We can take them."

I heard her paddle swooshing behind me, and I tried to match her strokes. But my paddle kept bumping Candi's, and she got more and more irritated.

Trin and Harmony had problems too, but of course they laughed about it. How did I end up with the drill sergeant for a partner?

Lamont and Cole reached the edge of the cove and turned around. They headed straight for us.

"It's not bumper boats!" I yelled.

"We are Viking warriors!" Lamont screamed.

Cole laughed an evil cackle and yelled, "Prepare to abandon your ship!"

When they got within a few feet, they turned a sharp right. They didn't knock us over, but they slapped the water with the flat sides of their paddles. Huge, heavy drops of salt water rained down on us.

Harmony and Trin zoomed in to join the splash war, yelling at the tops of their lungs. Candi laughed and fought back, soaking me more than anyone in the other kayaks.

I shook my head. The moment Trin and Harmony got close by, I yelled, "You said kayaking was quiet and peaceful."

"What?" Trin yelled back. "I can't hear you. What did you say?"

I rolled my eyes and mumbled, "Exactly."

The guys pulled ahead again, paddling toward the edge of the cove. Harmony and Trin fell in behind them.

"Can we leave the cove?" Lamont yelled back over his shoulder.

"Yeah," Candi answered. "As long as we hug the shoreline and don't go too far."

We paddled along behind them. Candi and I finally got a system down. "Hey, let's go a little slower," I told her. "I love them, but I really need some quiet right now."

"Sure," she answered. And I think she really got it, because she didn't even talk. We drifted along, and soon they got far enough ahead that we could hardly hear them. I looked at the shoreline and then at the ocean that stretched all the way to the blue sky.

I took a few deep breaths and had just started to relax when I heard someone behind us say, "Passing on your left."

I jumped. I hadn't even heard the tiniest splash. I turned around and saw two older girls in a kayak.

"Sorry," the one in front said softly. She pushed a strand of blonde hair from her eyes as they passed us. "It almost seems like a sin to talk out here, but I didn't want to scare you."

After they pulled in front of us with smooth, even strokes, the girl in back turned around. "Aren't you a Chosen Girl?" she asked.

"She's the drummer," Candi bragged. "Mello is amazing on drums."

"You really are," the girl agreed, her dark brown eyes shining. "I'd love to play the drums. They're so ... elemental."

When she said *elemental*, it sounded like the greatest compliment I'd ever gotten. Not the way Trin would have made it sound.

They slowed down until we were beside them again, and the blonde one said, "I'm Anna. I'm sure you have fans bugging you all the time. I don't want to be obnoxious, but thanks for doing morning assembly. It's the best music we've ever had."

I said, "No ..."

"Really!" the dark-eyed girl agreed. "I've never seen people so into it."

"But they aren't!" I exclaimed. "No one sang. I thought everyone hated us."

"Everyone hates *mornings*," she corrected. "But they love the music. Give it a few days, and they might even sing along." She smiled again. "I'm Emily."

"I guess you know I'm Mello. This is Candi. Her dad's the caretaker for Surf & Sand City," I said, jerking a thumb toward the back of my kayak.

"I don't see how you play in front of so many people," Anna said. "I would die of stage fright. I'd rather read a book."

"I made her come out here," Emily admitted. "But isn't it peaceful?" She held her oar with one hand and waved the other hand around at the shore and the ocean.

I laughed. "Yeah. I came out here to escape all the noise."

Anna blushed. "And we came and ruined it! I'm so sorry!"

I shook my head. "No, I didn't mean that ..." I felt myself blush too.

"Hey, if you need an escape, you should try the Quiet Waters Spa. It's beautiful," Emily said. "Soft music, pedicures, facials ..."

Anna added, "It's right across the street from the retreat center. Why don't you meet us there this afternoon? Two o'clock."

"I'd love to," I heard myself say.

Emily said, "Great. And now we'll leave you alone."

They pulled ahead again, and I sat smiling and paddling lazily, looking forward to chilling out at the Quiet Waters Spa.

A clanging bell interrupted my thoughts. "That's the bell for lunch," Candi said. "We better head back."

It took a while (and more coaching from Candi), but we got turned around.

She forgot about the quiet thing and talked all the way back. Once, when she stopped to breathe, I said, "Um, listen … about the spa: Don't mention it to Harmony and Trin, OK? Because they'll want to come, and it will turn into one big party, and that's not the point."

"Yeah. I'll cover for you," she offered.

"Thanks."

Back at the dock, Candi said, "I'll get the wire."

I noticed Karson on the dock.

"Let me," I offered, feeling athletic and confident. I even waved and called out, "Hey, Karson!"

"Do you know where Cole is?" he asked.

"Yeah," I answered, trying to flash him a charming grin. "He's on a kayak with Lamont. They should be back soon." I reached up for the wire and undid my seat strap. I stood up to get a better grip.

"No," Candi said, "don't stand —"

Splash. I tumbled into the cold water, and my life jacket popped me back up to the surface. I spluttered and spit as I came up, my hair plastered onto my face. I grabbed two handfuls and felt like I was peering through old-fashioned drapes on a picture window.

Karson walked toward me on the dock. He held a hand out to me, laughing. "I'd call this a rescue, but you aren't exactly in danger," he said as he tried to pull me onto the wooden platform.

My wet hand slipped from his grasp, and I fell into the water again. It took three more tries before I flopped onto the dock, feeling awkward and ugly and stupid. The closest I'd been to Karson in months, and I didn't even want to look into those root-beer brown eyes.

I looked around to make sure Candi was okay. She was. I mumbled, "Like I said, Cole should be back soon," and I practically ran to the cabin to change for lunch.

...

chapter 5

Everyone made it to the dining hall before lunch ended.

"What's with the wet hair?" Harmony asked.

Harmony would think Karson's rescue sounded romantic, but I knew the truth and didn't want to talk about it. "I felt like taking a shower," I answered. True. I had quickly washed the salt water off before putting on dry clothes.

Thankfully, no one asked for more details. "So didn't you love kayaking?" Trin asked. "Sorry we got so far ahead."

I tried to smile. "I didn't mind getting left behind. Yeah, kayaking is excellent. Well, mostly excellent."

"I'm glad we got our outdoor adventure in early today, because you know what we need to do next," Harmony said.

Trin sighed. "Practice. Surely we can do better tomorrow morning. I still think we need to do fun songs."

"What if you do a combination?" Lamont asked. "Something fun to start off and get everyone singing, and then some of Harmony's 'real' songs."

Trin nodded and so did Harmony. "Makes sense to me," I said. "And I think we need to avoid giving anything too much personality. They can't follow us."

"Sí. What works for concerts doesn't work the same when we're leading a group of people," Harmony agreed.

We finished eating and walked to the auditorium. We decided on five songs to run through and got warmed up. Candi slipped into the back of the building and pointed to her wrist. I flipped my phone open and checked the time: *1:45*.

We hadn't even played a song yet. No way would they let me leave. But the Quiet Waters Spa beckoned.

I couldn't explain why I wanted to go without them. They'd get their feelings hurt. Besides, they just didn't understand my need for quiet. The thought of Anna and Emily waiting at the spa while I sat stuck behind my drums made my stomach hurt.

Aha!

I grabbed my belly and groaned. "I'm sorry," I said. "I don't feel too well. I think I'm going to have to skip out on practice."

Harmony walked over. "What's wrong? Your stomach?" she asked, totally concerned.

I nodded and said, "Yeah. I think I'll be OK if I get some rest."

"We could all use some downtime," Trin agreed. "How about we go back to the cabin and sit around and chat? We can practice later."

I groaned again. "I better go alone. You go ahead with practice and fill me in later."

Harmony shook her head. "I hate to send you off by your-self. It hit pretty fast, didn't it?"

I looked at her face. Was that a challenge? No, just worry.

"I'll walk her over," Candi volunteered. "I'll make sure she's all settled, and then I'll let her rest."

I smiled a truly grateful smile. "Thanks, Candi. That sounds perfect."

I stepped into the spa and knew immediately this place was what I needed. Even with shoes on, I felt my feet sink into the superthick carpet. I closed my eyes and breathed in the scents of vanilla and cinnamon. Soft piano music floated through the air.

I heard Anna's voice, barely more than a whisper. "This is Mello, the one we were waiting for."

I opened my eyes and saw a tiny woman in a white lab coat smiling at me. "Then we begin," she said simply, motion-ing for us to follow. Anna and Emily walked behind her toward the back wall. I turned around to thank Candi, try-ing to think of a polite way to tell her to leave. But she had already gone. Excellent.

We sat in a row of soft chairs, and three women came for-ward to do our pedicures. Hot water, lotion, and strong but gentle hands rubbing my feet almost put me to sleep. No, it was better than sleep: I felt totally relaxed, but still knew everything that was going on around me.

It amazed me that Anna and Emily could sit so long with-out talking. Harmony and Trin would have needed to com-ment on everything—from the temperature of the water to the artwork on the wall.

When my turn came to pick a color of nail polish, I chose an almost-pink gloss. I waited for Anna and Emily to tease me. *What's the point? If you choose such a light color, no one will even know you got your toes done. Why not hot pink or purple?*

Instead, Emily said, "Oh, do you mind if I use that color too?"

By the time I paid, said good-bye to Anna and Emily, and walked toward my cabin, I felt ready to take on the world. I ran into Trin and Harmony near the Snack Shack.

"Ohwow, you look better!" Trin said. "I guess that rest did you good."

Harmony gave me a shoulder squeeze and added, "After practice, we stayed out here so we wouldn't bother you. Are you OK?"

I hugged them both. "Better than OK. Thanks."

• • •

Saturday Evening

We ate dinner together and went to the evening assembly. Candi scooted into a seat beside me, and I whispered, "Thanks for earlier."

I noticed everyone—or almost everyone—sang along with Caleb, the music guy. That bothered me. So they didn't like mornings. Who cares? If they could sing with Caleb, they should be able to sing with us.

I reminded myself that Anna and Emily liked our music. But they probably just said that to be nice.

The speaker talked about servanthood again. We didn't whisper or text-message, but my mind wandered a little. I worried about the music. I didn't want to look stupid again in the morning. Then I got mad about worrying. This retreat was supposed to be the one week of the year when I didn't have to worry about anything.

By the time assembly ended, my happy-feet feelings had pretty much worn off. And when Harmony suggested another practice . . . *poof!* Every last shred of peacefulness vanished.

I stomped to the front of the auditorium and took my place behind the drums. "What's the first song?" I demanded.

"Um, 'Give Me Oil in My Lamp,'" Harmony answered.

Trin smiled and held her hands out, turning an imaginary steering wheel. "And we're going to invite people onstage to sing different verses into the mike—you know, 'Give me gas in my Ford, keep me truckin' for the Lord.'"

Lamont laughed and sang, "Give me wax on my board, keep me surfin' for the Lord," while he swayed back and forth, pretending to surf.

Candi jumped up and high-fived Lamont. Then she sang, "Give me music on my iPod, keep me singing praises to God."

"Give me hot sauce on my taco. Make me macho, macho, macho!" Harmony belted through her nose.

"I've got it!" I yelled. "Can we just work out the music without singing all four hundred verses tonight?"

Harmony looked like I had slapped her. "What's your deal?" she asked.

I rolled my eyes. "You can't figure it out? The time after evening assembly is like the funnest time at retreat. It's when everyone has pillow fights and plays flashlight wars and everything else cool, and I'm stuck in here playing my stinking drums. I'm sick of practicing, OK? I'm missing the whole retreat because of the Chosen Girls."

Harmony made her confused face. "Mello, please! You've never once been in a pillow fight or flashlight war at retreat. You always sit in the room and read."

I spit out, "Well, at least before I always had the option, didn't I? But not this year. No. I have to practice. I knew once Trin and the band got involved, the retreat would be ruined."

Trin's face turned as pink as her hair. "If you had been at practice this afternoon, we could *all* be having fun right now! We practiced while you rested, Mello. Tonight's practice is for *you*. So quit griping at us."

Lamont coughed into his fist. "All right, then, I think everyone is agreed that we should get through this practice as quickly as possible. 'Give Me Oil in My Lamp.' Mello?"

I set the beat, and we played the song. And the other four songs. No one talked more than they had to, and no one goofed around.

The Chosen Girls had never had such an efficient practice.

Or such a boring one.

By the time we left the auditorium, all the fun on the grounds had ended. No one ran around shooting water guns; no one was screaming. Nothing.

We walked to the cabin without saying a word. Even Candi, who followed me, was quiet. When we got to the door, she said, "Well, see you in the morning, Mello."

I said, "Yeah, sure," and shut the door.

I unzipped my suitcase and reached for my pj's.

"Hey, Mello," Trin said. "I'm so sorry about what I said. About your missing practice. That wasn't fair—I mean, it's not like you got sick on purpose."

"Sí, I feel bad too. You were stuck in here, miserable, all afternoon. That must have been *so* boring. No wonder you wanted to get out and do something fun tonight," Harmony added.

"And we had so much fun thinking of dumb verses to songs this afternoon! I wish you had been there," Trin said, throwing an arm around my shoulders.

Harmony nodded. "That probably made you feel left out tonight, when we sang them. Do you forgive us?"

Did I forgive them? I skipped practice to get a pedicure, yelled at them for having fun, and now they asked *me* to forgive *them*?

"Uh, sure," I mumbled.

Harmony asked, "How's your stomach feel tonight? You're holding it again."

"Um, yeah," I answered. "Actually, it just started hurting again."

...

chapter 6

The next morning's service went better. It surprised me how
many people wanted to come onstage and sing into the mike.
Even the cool people who always sit in the back row got into it.
Obviously, not everyone has my hang-ups about performing.

We heard, "Give me programs on my laptop. Keep me typing till I drop," and "Give me new games on my Xbox, 'cause
I think it really rocks." And about ten other verses. Everyone
laughed the whole time, and when we started our next song,
a lot of people sang with us. Not Makayla and the Snob Mob,
of course, and that got on my nerves. If I had to be happy
and singing, it seemed like everyone should have to.

After assembly, I overheard Karson talking to Hunter. "Hey,
wanna Rollerblade?"

That's it! I thought. *I'll make up for yesterday by doing
something fun with Trin and Harmony today. And if I happen
to see Karson ... well, that will be a bonus.*

I found them at the sound booth with Lamont. "Let's go Rollerblading!" I announced.

Trin and Harmony turned to me with open mouths. They looked at each other. "What? Did she just say Rollerblading?" Harmony asked Trin.

"I thought so," Trin answered, pretending to clean out her ear. "I must be having hearing problems."

Lamont shoved both of them. "Mello's trying to branch out here. Go with it!"

Harmony smiled. "Right! Come on."

We got our gear from the Sports Shack and found a bench to sit on. I pulled off my shoes and looked nervously at my pile of equipment. "The fact that the Rollerblades come with a helmet, elbow pads, wrist pads, and knee pads makes me a little nervous," I admitted.

Trin snapped the last fastener on her second Rollerblade closed and stood up. "You'll be fine," she said as she raced down the sidewalk, did a perfect turn, and raced back. She stopped inches from me. "Come on, Mello! Whose idea was this, anyway?"

I finally got my stuff on and stood up. My ankles caved in and my knees buckled. "Oh, I can't do this," I wailed. "What was I thinking?"

"It's easier once you get going," Harmony said, zooming ahead.

I tried to imitate them as I followed along behind. My legs felt like rubber by the time I got fifteen feet, and then I hit a rock. More of a pebble, really. I landed soundly on my backside. Trin and Harmony sped back and helped me up.

Ten feet later it happened again.

The next time, I managed to go at least thirty feet before I fell. "I have pads for every part of my body except the part I keep landing on," I complained as I sat in the middle of the sidewalk.

"There's a hill ahead," Harmony said. "It's easier going down."

I laughed. "I've done nothing but go down since we started," I reminded her. As I crawled onto my knees and then struggled to stand, I thought, *It's a good thing I* haven't *seen Karson. He must be miles ahead.*

I stood at the top of the hill and watched Harmony and Trin fly down it and around the bend. I considered sitting on the grass, enjoying the perfect weather and the gorgeous scenery. Or I could take off the Rollerblades and walk back to the Sports Shack. Nope, neither plan would work. They would come find me.

I had to try.

I took a deep breath and counted. *One. Two. Three.* Then I pushed off and started down the hill.

It didn't take long to see I only needed to keep my skates straight and coast. Harmony was right! Going downhill was way easier than skating on level ground.

The wind blew my hair out of my face. I bent my knees a little and leaned over them. As I neared the curve, I pretended to be a speed skater or a downhill skier in the —

Bike! Crossing the path. Have to stop — can't stop —

Ouch.

"Idiot!"

I recognized Makayla's voice and then her angry face, looking down at me.

"I could have broken my neck. What were you thinking, skating right into the bike path like that?" she yelled.

I blinked up at her and thought, *Don't cry. Yeah, your ankle hurts, but don't cry*.

"Shoulda known it was a Chosen Girl," Makayla continued, her hands on her hips. "She thinks she owns the path—probably the whole retreat center—because they're doing music. Big whoop."

"Are you hurt?" Harmony asked as she and Trin skated up beside Makayla.

Makayla tossed her short hair. "No, but I could have been. Easily."

Trin said, "Harmony was talking to Mello. The person sprawled out on the sidewalk. The one you would have run over, Makayla, if she hadn't sacrificed herself to save you from getting hurt." She knelt beside me. "Are you all right?"

I said, "I think so. A couple of strawberries. And my ankle hurts a little."

"Too bad it's not her wrist. Then we wouldn't have to suffer through her lame drumming," Makayla said. She got back on her bike, and she and her followers left.

"Let's go to first aid," Trin said. "But first let me see your ankle." She carefully unbuckled my skates and gently peeled off my sock.

"It looks OK. You probably just twisted it, but it would be smart to put ice on it."

I nodded and started taking off the other skate.

"Your toenails look pretty," Trin commented.

I froze.

"They do," Harmony said. "Wow. They're painted."

I nodded.

"You never paint your toenails," she continued.

My heart started beating double-time. "I thought, uh, for the retreat . . . it might be nice," I said.

"But they weren't painted on the bus on the way up. I remember. Did you actually pack nail polish, Mello? I'm proud of you!" Harmony grinned at me.

"Hey, I know!" Trin said. "Let's bandage Mello's wounds and get her back to the cabin. Then, while she's icing her ankle, Harmony and I can paint *our* toenails. We'll all match!"

I looked at the sidewalk. I swallowed. I felt a tiny trickle of sweat form on my forehead and run down my face. "I didn't bring nail polish," I said.

"Huh?" Harmony asked. "I don't get it."

I took a deep breath before I admitted, "My stomach really did hurt yesterday. I promise. And I did rest. I just didn't rest at the cabin. I rested at a . . . spa."

"A spa?" Trin blurted out. "There's a spa here? And you went alone?"

"And didn't take us?" Harmony asked.

I nodded.

"Oh. She couldn't take us, Harmony," Trin explained. "We were stuck practicing our stinkin' guitars. Remember? Like Mello said. Missing the whole retreat because of the Chosen Girls."

Harmony looked at me with big, sad eyes. "And I felt sorry for you. Well, I don't anymore. You can get your own ice pack. Let's go, Trin."

They skated away.

I felt a twinge of guilt.

Wait a minute, I thought. *I'm not the guilty one here. This retreat was supposed to be all about relaxing. Why are they making me feel bad about one measly pedicure? Because they're only thinking of* themselves, *that's why.*

I watched them go before I gathered up my skates and stood up. I winced.

I wasn't sure what hurt more—my ankle or my heart.

•••

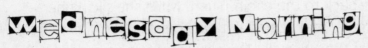 Wednesday Morning

Candi found me after Wednesday-morning assembly. "Will you teach me something on the drums, Mello? Please," she asked.

I looked at Harmony and Trin. I tried to beg them with my eyes, *Please rescue me.*

"Perfect timing, Candi," Harmony said. "We're going surfing this morning, and Mello hates to surf. Plus, her ankle probably still hurts."

Trin called across the auditorium, "Cole, Karson, Hunter—we'll meet you at the beach in fifteen." She turned to me. "Have fun with the drum lessons, Mello." Then she left, with Harmony right behind her.

Lamont turned off the soundboard. "Catch ya later, Mello," he said, heading for the door.

I grabbed his arm. "Lamont, please," I whispered.

He shook his head. "I would if I could, but you've dissed my playing enough for me to know I can't help with drum lessons."

"But Trin and Harmony ... they're being twits ...," I began.

He looked into my eyes and said, "You did that to yourself, Mello." Then he walked out and let the door bang shut behind him.

Candi put her hands together to plead. "So is it a yes?" she asked. "I'm probably no good, but I want to learn so much. And if anyone can teach me, you can, 'cause you're incredible."

"Tell my friends that," I mumbled, limping toward the stage. She didn't follow me. "What are you waiting for?" I asked. "Let's get started."

She squealed and ran all the way to the drum set. She grabbed my sticks and started pounding everything — snares, toms, cymbals. I covered my ears and made myself count to three (no way I could make it to ten) before I yelled, "Please stop!"

She didn't hear me, but she finally looked up. I guess the look on my face (and my hands over my ears) must have been easy to understand. After one more cymbal crash, she froze.

"You didn't ask for a free-for-all on my set, Candi. You said you wanted to learn something."

She hung her head. "I'm sorry. I've dreamed about playing for so long that I thought it might come naturally." She peeked up at me through her eyelashes. "Did it sound kind of good?"

Poor kid. "Um, that last crash was nice," I managed. "Listen, I've never really taught anyone to play, so you'll have to be patient with me."

"Sure! No prob. I'm just so happy you're going to teach me. Maybe I can play with you guys before you leave!"

"Whoa there, Candi. That's setting your sights pretty high," I said, shaking my head. "How about you start by giving me a strong backbeat?"

"OK. What's a backbeat?" she asked.

I buried my face in my hands and moaned, "This is going to be harder than I thought."

chapter • 7

...

"Didn't you say your mom makes you take piano?" I asked.

She frowned. "Yeah. I hate piano."

"But did you know a lot of schools require two years of piano for any kid who wants to be in the percussion section?"

"Nuh-uh!"

"Uh-huh," I said with a nod. "So stick with those lessons. They'll help a ton. Like, do you know what four-four time is?"

"Yeah. That means four beats to a measure, doesn't it? Most songs are in four-four."

"Excellent! Where did you learn that?" I asked.

She rolled her eyes. "Piano."

"See, your lessons are already paying off. Now, the back-beat happens on beats two and four. It's the absolute key.

Everything the band does is based on the drummer laying a good, solid, consistent backbeat," I explained. "I'll count one, two, three, four. You tap the snare on beats two and four. Ready? One, *two*, three, *four.*"

I stopped and closed my eyes. I breathed in and out, slowly. "Well, that was close," I said softly. "Let's try again. You're going to tap the snare on beats *two* and *four.* You need to hit right on the beat—not early or late. Ready? One, *two*, three, *four.*"

I felt my whole self shudder as she missed both beats again.

"Um, OK, that's the first step. Now I'm going to play some music. You clap with beats two and four. You should be able to hear the dominating snare sound on the recording," I explained. "How about you step away from my drums? I mean, come down here closer to the speaker."

"So I'm already getting it, huh? Am I learning pretty fast?" she asked.

I smiled. "You're the best student I've ever had."

Candi couldn't find the beat on the recorded music, either. I clapped with her, but that didn't help. We listened to the same song three times, and she still couldn't get it.

"This is fun and all," she said, "but I want to learn to play the drums. Rolls and crashes and syncopated rhythms."

I had to bite the inside of my bottom lip to keep from saying what I wanted to say. *You want to learn to play the drums. I want to go to the beach and watch Karson surf. Neither of us is getting our wish today, unless . . .*

"I need that bongo I played in Russia!" I blurted out.

Candi said, "I've got a little drum—a wooden one from Mexico. I never use it. I mean, it's not anything like your drums."

"Get it and meet me at the beach, where everyone's surfing," I told her.

"Surfing?" she asked. "Why there?"

"We need to hear the steady pounding of the surf, because you're ready for the next lesson. It's called 'Rhythm of the Sea.'"

•••

I found a spot under two palm trees with a bit of shade and—more important—a great view of the surfers. Trin and Harmony seemed to be having a good time, and I spotted Karson paddling out. He found his wave and had just pulled up on his board when Candi appeared.

She stuck the drum in my face. "Will this work?" she asked.

I took it and looked at the striped wooden base and the leather drumhead. "It's perfect!" I declared, giving it a few taps. "This is actually an excellent little drum. But you don't get to use it yet. Stretch out on the sand, close your eyes, and listen to the waves crashing."

She sat back and closed her eyes. "I don't see how this is going to help. I live here. I hear the ocean every day," she complained.

"Exactly!" I agreed. "You hear it. But you don't *listen* to it. You aren't listening now. You're talking."

She sat quietly for a minute, and I watched Karson. Why hadn't I thought of this earlier?

Then she opened her eyes and said, "Hey! You don't have *your* eyes closed."

"I'm not the student," I reminded her.

I enjoyed a few more minutes of peace before I said, "Now you get to use the drum. Watch the waves and listen to them. Hit the drum each time a wave hits the beach."

She actually did pretty well with that.

"Now only hit it on every other wave."

She did that too.

I smiled at her and said, "That, darling, is a backbeat. Congratulations!"

We started making up songs that went with the rhythm of the sea — songs about the ocean and the beach and the seabirds calling. She and I took turns playing the drum while we sang.

Then Candi closed her eyes again and started singing a song about missing someone so much that nothing else mattered. It broke my heart.

"Who's that song for, Candi?" I asked.

She kept her eyes closed, but a tear escaped from under her lashes. "My little sister."

My heart seemed to stop. "What happened?"

"She died last year — leukemia."

"Oh, Candi," I breathed. I reached for her and hugged her hard. "I know what it's like to lose someone."

"I thought so. I don't know how, but I could tell," she answered. Now tears ran freely down her freckled cheeks. "Mattie was my best friend. We did everything together." Candi looked out over the ocean, but she didn't seem to see it. "It's been eleven months, and I still feel lost without her."

"Oh, sweetie. It hasn't even been a year?" I asked. "I think you're holding up really well."

"Sometimes," she agreed. "Sometimes not. I remember the first time I made it through a whole day without crying. As I got ready for bed I thought, 'I haven't cried today!' Then I felt so guilty about enjoying myself without her that I cried all night!" She laughed, and I laughed with her, wiping my own tears away.

"I think about the times I fought with her over the stupidest stuff. Whose turn with the iPod, whose turn to choose the DVD for movie night. Why did I act like getting my way mattered more to me than she did?"

"Because you're a normal kid. And so was she," I answered. "You can't go through life beating yourself up over that stuff, Candi."

"It gets worse. Can you believe I even felt jealous of her cancer sometimes? How sick is that? But everyone paid attention to her. Sometimes I felt like I didn't matter anymore. Like it would be easier to be the one in the hospital bed than the one who had to keep going to school, keep smiling, keep acting like . . . like I wasn't dying too—on the inside." She wiped her eyes with the back of her hand.

"You aren't awful, Candi. Those are normal feelings," I assured her.

"Well, anyway, I told her I was sorry before she died. For everything."

"That must have been hard—but excellent," I said. "Having that chance to say good-bye." I felt my own tears falling harder now. "I didn't get to."

She caught her breath. "I'm sorry, Mello. I've talked on and on. I . . . I didn't even ask who *you* lost."

"That's OK. Really. I don't talk about it."

"But you need to," Candi insisted. "Don't hold all that pain inside. It only makes it worse."

I shook my head.

Candi traced a finger through the sand. "Do you ever catch yourself hoping you were wrong? That it didn't really happen?" she whispered. I leaned closer to hear her over the surf. "You know—that you dreamed it or something?"

"You do that too?" I asked, blinking in surprise. "Maybe that's why I don't talk about it. Talking about it makes it too real." I leaned back and looked at the clouds floating past, wishing Candi and I could hop on one and ride away from all the pain. "I never lost that feeling you're talking about. It gets smaller—comes less often, maybe. But there's still a part of me that thinks one day I'll walk into the living room and see my brother sitting there. He'll say, 'Ha! Got you,' and laugh. Then things will be like they used to be."

Candi wrapped her chubby arms around me for a quick hug. "Thank you for telling me," she said. "It helps to know I'm not the only one. I'm not crazy after all."

I had to lighten the mood. I punched her arm. "Oh, you're crazy all right," I said.

"What does that make you?" she asked with a giggle.

"Crazier," I answered.

Her face turned serious again. "Mello, they aren't coming back. We have to face it and move on."

I nodded. "I know, Candi."

Trin ran up the beach. "Did you see that, Mello?" she yelled.

"What?"

Harmony came behind Trin and said, "Karson just caught a major wave—the biggest one all day. He rode it right to the beach. Didn't you hear us screaming?"

"No, I've been kinda busy with drum lessons," I answered.

Candi blushed. "I'm sorry, Mello. I shouldn't have wasted your whole morning."

I put my hand over hers and said, "This morning wasn't wasted, Candi. I'm glad I spent it with you."

•••

During lunch, the guys sat at our table again. Karson said, "Missed ya during surfing, Mello."

"Thanks. I heard you did great," I answered, losing myself in those eyes. My stomach tightened. *Crud*, I thought. *At this rate, I'll never get to eat.* I forced myself to look away from his gorgeous grin long enough to choke down some salad.

Everyone around me relived their best wave, their worst wipeout, and biggest nosedive. I just listened until Karson said, "After lunch, how about KCH takes on the Chosen Girls in Frisbee golf?"

Trin shook her head. "Sounds fun, but we better practice."

"We don't need to practice. We're great at Frisbee!" I said.

"Not Frisbee," Trin corrected. "I mean we need to get ready for—ouch! Harmony! Did you just kick me?"

Harmony smiled sweetly at Trin and winked at me. Then she turned to Cole and asked, "The question is, boys, are you ready for us?"

Cole laughed. "What? Are you like pros or something?"

"You'll find out," Harmony answered with a confident nod.

•••

"OK, so have either of you ever played Frisbee golf?" Harmony whispered as we followed Karson and Cole to the course.

Trin groaned. "Harmony, you told them we're pros!"

"Did not. I said they'd find out."

Trin looked at me and said, "Well, you told them we're good, Mello."

"Good at Frisbee," I corrected. "I didn't say good at Frisbee golf."

When we got there Cole asked, "Lamont, which team are you playing on?"

"Ours!" I said quickly. "He's a Chosen Girl all the way."

"I wish we could do something about that name," Lamont grumbled, rolling his eyes.

Harmony whined, "Please, Lamont, we really need you!"

He grinned. "What can I say? The women need me."

Hunter brought seven brightly colored Frisbees from the Sports Shack. Harmony grabbed purple, Trin got pink, and I got light blue. "Anyone got a coin?" Karson asked as Hunter passed out the rest of the Frisbees. "We need to flip to see who goes first."

"Oh, we'll let you go first," Harmony offered. "You'll need every advantage we can give you." After the guys walked to the first tee, she whispered, "This way we can see how to play."

Each guy threw toward the hole. They declared Hunter's throw the best. Then they looked at us.

"Guess that means it's our turn," Trin said, stepping up to the tee. Her Frisbee actually got pretty close to Hunter's.

"Cool frijoles! Told ya to watch out, guys!" Harmony crooned. She teed up and threw her Frisbee straight into a tree.

Cole laughed. "Watch out is right. With throws that out of control, you might take a head off."

Harmony just laughed along with him.

I stepped up next. Why had I agreed to this? Yeah, I could watch Karson ... but everyone else could watch me. Watch me make a fool of myself.

Sure enough, my Frisbee caught the wind and came almost back to my feet.

"G'day, mate!" Hunter called. "Are you from Australia, Mello? Trying to turn this into a boomerang toss?"

I managed to follow Harmony's example and laugh along with everyone else.

Lamont came through for us, besting Hunter's throw.

"Ohwow, we won!" Trin yelled. "We got closest!"

"No one's 'holed out' yet. Now each team throws from their team's best landing, until someone gets it in the hole," Karson explained. "But I'm sure you knew that, since you're practically professionals."

"Um, sure," Harmony said with a grin.

The game took all afternoon. We got better as we went along, but without Lamont it wouldn't have even been close. He yelled, "The mighty Lamont scores again!" or "Just call me La-marvelous!" after every throw.

After all eleven holes, KCH won by three strokes. They jumped around bonking fists, high-fiving, and pounding one another on the back. Cole sang, "We Are the Champions," at the top of his lungs.

When they finally calmed down, Karson said, "I'll take the KCH Frisbees back. Mello, can you grab the ones from the Chosen Girls?"

"What's the matter, Karson?" Lamont teased. "Those four extra Frisbees too heavy for you?"

Karson blushed.

I said, "I'll get them," and quickly grabbed Harmony's and Trin's. Lamont wouldn't let go of his, so I had to twist it loose then whack him on the head with it before I left with Karson.

Once I was walking beside him, I couldn't think of anything to say. *Please!* I told myself. *It's not that hard. He's just a guy like Lamont. Except he's so cute and he has that lopsided grin and he's in a band . . .*

"Good game," I finally blurted out.

At the exact same time, Karson said something.

We both said, "What?" Then we started laughing.

"You first," he said.

I blushed. "I just said, 'Good game.'" It sounded even more stupid the second time. "What did you say?"

"I said, 'Anyone could tell you're a drummer,'" he answered. "Are you always beating out a rhythm?"

I looked down at my right hand, tapping away on the stack of Frisbees in my left. "Especially when I'm nerv—um, I mean, yeah. Can't stop the beat."

We got to the Sports Shack and waited at the counter. The service window was open, but the worker must have been in back. "So what's your little sister's name?" Karson asked.

I looked sideways at him. "I don't have a little sister."

"Who's the redhead that's been hanging with you all week?"

I laughed. "Oh, that's Candi. Her parents run this place, and for some reason, she's attached herself to me. She's the reason I missed surfing this morning—I can't seem to get away from her." I peeked in the window and called, "Hello? Is anyone in there?"

Karson leaned on the counter and said, "We can't leave until we sign these Frisbees back in. I don't know what's taking so long."

I heard footsteps. Then Candi stepped to the window.

Her face looked all red and blotchy, like she'd been crying.

chapter • 8

...

"Sorry it took so long," Candi mumbled. "I had to count the volleyballs in back."

Karson looked at Candi's face, then at me. "Uh, I'll let you check these in, Mello. Later." He shoved the Frisbees at me and walked away.

My stomach twisted and turned like it was on its own personal roller-coaster ride. Had Candi heard me? Probably.

But what if she hadn't? Maybe she'd been crying about something else. If I apologized for something she didn't even know about, it would only make things worse. I'd already gotten myself into trouble with Harmony and Trin because of the spa. I didn't need Candi mad at me too.

I handed her the Frisbees and said, "There are seven." While she found the paper and checked them off, I frantically analyzed the situation. *What, exactly, had I said? Something about Candi always hanging around. Had I said it in a mean way? Or maybe I said it in a nice way — like "I've enjoyed spending a lot of time with her." No, I didn't think I said it quite like that. Oh, I wished I had!*

And how loud did I say it? Probably not too loud. Karson had been right beside me. Maybe it was almost a whisper. And it would help if I said it facing Karson. Then most of the sound might have stayed outside the Sport Shack. Or did I say it right into the window? I thought I might have.

The details that seemed so important fled my brain. How would I know if she was upset because of me? I could ask, "What's wrong?" but ... did I really want to know?

I decided to hope for the best. When Candi said, "OK, you're all checked in," I just smiled at her and said, "Thanks, Candi. Have a great day!" Then I walked away, like everything was fine.

But my rolling stomach said otherwise.

• • •

Thursday Morning

At the end of morning assembly on Thursday, Mr. Karuthers bounded onto the stage. "I've got exciting news to share!" he said. "This year, for the first time ever, our retreat includes a service project. We don't want to just talk about servant-hood, we want to live it out.

"You'll be divided into teams for this project, based on cabin number. Teams A, B, and C come from cabins one through forty. You'll meet with your team leaders in the back of the auditorium. After a brief training session, your leaders will bus you to nearby urban areas, where you will pick up litter and sweep the sidewalks.

"Teams D, E, and F come from cabins forty-one through eighty. These teams will be trained in the cafeteria. Then they will take sandwiches or blankets to homeless people.

"Everyone who participates will receive a pair of gloves with 'Philippians 2:5 – 7 Servant Attitude' printed on them." He held up a pair. "These gloves are white. I hope they aren't white when you get in tonight. Got it? This is what it's about. Let's get out there and get our hands — well, our gloves — dirty!"

"Excellent!" I said, looking for our team leader. "I love this. A chance to be a real servant."

"Yeah," Trin agreed. "I wish we could do it."

"What do you mean?" I asked.

Harmony sighed. "If only we hadn't goofed off all day yesterday. The concert's coming up, and we haven't even discussed what songs we're doing."

"We tried at the shed, before we even left home," I reminded her. "But you were more excited about packing."

Harmony said, "Don't make an issue of it, Mello. Trin's right. We've got to stay here and practice today. This concert on the beach is going to be huge! We need to rock. Besides, don't tell me you really want to pick up trash. Or talk to strangers — *homeless* strangers! You can't even ask the workers in the grocery store where the baking soda is."

I crossed my arms and slumped into a seat, waiting for everyone else to clear out of the auditorium. So we could practice. Again.

How am I supposed to be a servant, I wondered, *when all I ever get to do is play the drums and babysit Candi? The rest of the campers are out there feeding the homeless, cleaning up the streets — really making a difference. I'd like a chance to do something big for God too.*

"So what's your opening song going to be?" Lamont asked, moving toward the sound booth.

"Before we talk about the order," Harmony said, "I have an idea. How about a song about the theme verses? We could sing it in morning assembly and at the concert."

"You mean write one? About the servant verses from Philippians?" Trin asked. "Ohwow, what a great idea."

Harmony turned to me, still hunkered down on my bench. "Mello? Any lyrics come to mind?"

A flood of words came to me:

I just need some me time — free time.
A moment-just-to-be time.
Time out with nothin' to prove.

But that didn't exactly fit the verses. *None that I can say out loud*, I thought. I shook my head.

Trin and Harmony traded looks. "OK, then, I guess it's up to us this time," Trin said. She opened her Bible to Philippians and read the verses. "It looks like attitude is the main thing," she said. "We're supposed to have the same attitude Jesus had."

"Yeah, God himself choosing to become a servant. Who are we to walk around thinking about ourselves?" Lamont added.

I thought, *This should be fun to watch. They don't have a clue how to write a song.* So far, I'd written most of the lyrics our band sang.

Harmony said, "I can't think of a single line."

I smirked.

"Let's pray," Trin suggested. They bowed their heads. "God, these verses in your Word are powerful. They're talking about something radical — a whole new way of thinking and living. Inspire us. Help us to write a song that will grip hearts and change lives. Amen."

As soon as they looked up, Harmony said, "How about, 'I want to live to serve you, show you I deserve you'?"

Trin smiled, whipped out her PDA, and started typing. "Way fabulous. Keep it coming!"

By the time we got to our instruments, I had to admit they'd done pretty well. It surprised me that Trin and Harmony, of all people, could write a song about servant-hood. I liked the line that said

When I lose direction —
need some reconnection —
then I find perfection in the light of you.

We ran through the song until we got it down. Then we talked about what other songs we wanted to do, and in what order. Well, *they* talked. I listened and nodded when they asked me questions. I sang because I had to, but I think I made it pretty clear I didn't want to be at practice.

"When are we changing to super suits?" Trin asked as we packed up.

Harmony looked at Lamont. "You won't be able to show the video, will you?"

"Not on the beach. We don't have equipment for that," he answered.

Trin twirled a strand of pink hair around her finger. "Without the video, changing into the suits will just be, like, a costume change. The video explains it all—that we aren't really any-thing amazing—we're just normal people who mess up."

"But when we pray," Harmony said, nodding, "amazing things happen. God transforms us. I love the way you showed that in the video, Lamont."

"Well, yeah, I'd call it a stroke of genius," he agreed.

"So the video is brilliant," I said. "It doesn't matter. We can't use it at the concert."

Harmony said, "Right. And I'm with Trin. I don't want to change clothes just to have a costume change. I want people to understand what the suits represent. How can we make this work?"

"What if we talked about it?" Trin asked. "Kinda told our story? How we struggled to get it together as a band."

"And how God changed us when we prayed!" Harmony exclaimed. "I love it. We could each say something—" She looked at me.

"No way," I said, shaking my head. "I'm doing well to 'hide behind my drums' up there, as you call it. Do you know what it would do to me to actually stand up onstage and talk? I'd never be able to do that."

She patted me on the shoulder. "That's what I figured. Don't worry about it. Trin and I can do the talking."

"How about before our new song?" Trin asked. "We're doing it last, right?"

Harmony said, "Sounds good to me."

They looked at me, and I shrugged. It wasn't my deal.

"Lamont, any ideas on lights?" Harmony asked. "Some way to make this cool?"

He started to grin. "Oh, yeah. How about I use a super-tight spotlight and zoom in on Trin's face while she's talking?

Meanwhile, Harmony and Mello go backstage and change. Then Harmony comes front and center to a marked spot, and I shine the spot on *her* face. There may be a little sunlight left, but not much by then. I think it will work — see?"

We stared at him.

He held his hands out. "Because I'm only showing her face, no one will know she already changed. When she finishes her speech, I cut the lights. You get in place, I flip the lights back on, and *kapow!* You're superheroes."

Harmony said, "Cool frijoles! Lamont, I love the way your brain works. That's why we let you hang with us, you know."

"Well, that," he agreed, "and my good looks, of course."

On the way out the door Harmony asked, "Hey, Mello, where's our number one fan?"

"Yeah," Trin added. "Candi hasn't missed a practice yet."

I shrugged. Like I was supposed to know where she was all the time? Please!

After practice, we went to our cabin. Harmony and Trin walked together, talking and laughing, and I followed them. When Trin opened the door, she screamed.

We stepped inside. The smell made me gag.

"It looks like someone emptied the trash bin on our floor!" Trin cried.

Harmony held her nose. "The lunchroom trash bin," she added. "Gross!"

"And look at our sleeping bags," I said, wading through garbage to get to my bed. I reached out to touch the slimy blue goop. "They squeezed toothpaste all over them."

Trin looked at hers. "No. They didn't do anything to my sleeping bag," she said with a sigh of relief.

"Mine either," Harmony added, sitting on her bed. "That's weird."

"They probably ran out of toothpaste," Trin suggested. She kicked at half a bean burrito. "Who would do this? Did we make someone mad?"

Harmony laughed. "I didn't think our music was *this* bad!"

I thought of Candi. If she did hear me complain about her, would she be upset enough to trash our room?

The toothpaste was on my bed. And only Candi knew which bed was mine. She hadn't come to watch practice ...

"It doesn't really matter who did it," I said. "We've got to clean it up."

"Mello, could you go find Candi?" Trin asked. "She probably knows where trash bags and all kinds of cleaning supplies are. And she's such a doll. She'd probably even help us."

Should I tell them Candi might have been the one who made the mess? But then I'd have to explain why. "Um, I want to start scrubbing my sleeping bag," I answered. "Then maybe it will dry by tonight."

Harmony said, "I'll go get her."

I dragged my sleeping bag onto the porch. I got toilet paper from the bathhouse and tried to wipe the toothpaste off with that. *Ewww.* It stuck to the goop in little white clumps. I got a stick, and that worked better for scraping off the biggest blobs. Then I used a wet washcloth to scrub the rest.

I wondered if Harmony had found Candi yet. And if Candi would admit to messing up our room. Would she tell Harmony why?

Trin walked past me, back and forth, carrying out armloads of garbage. "Don't scrub too hard," she said. "That minty-fresh scent is the best thing we've got going right now. Leave some of it to cover up the stench."

Harmony came back loaded with trash bags, paper towels, and disinfectant spray. "I couldn't find Candi, but I found a really nice janitor. He said he'd come if we need him to," she said.

I left my sleeping bag stretched over a chair and went in to help.

"You know this is your fault, Mello," Trin said.

I stiffened, a dirty napkin in one hand and a handful of tortilla chips in the other. "Why?" I asked.

She smiled. "You're the one who was so mad we didn't get to clean up litter today. Someone probably just did this so we wouldn't feel left out."

"I bet the Snob Mob did it," Harmony said. "Makayla is mad as anything about our being onstage this week. And this garbage," she said, dumping handfuls into the bag, "just reeks of her."

"What a joke that she's mad about the music," Trin said. "Can you imagine Makayla and her gang leading worship music? With their attitudes?" She looked at me and then looked away quickly.

What?

"I hope it was Makayla," I said. "You're right, Harmony. They seem a lot more likely to do this than … um, I mean … remember? I almost made Makayla have a bike wreck. Maybe that's why she put toothpaste on my bed."

"That's right! Well, I think we got all the trash," Harmony said as she tied the bag closed. "If we scrub the floors with paper towels and spray enough disinfectant, we might be able to breathe in here."

Trin leaned over to look under her bed. "Wait! There's a half-eaten brownie we missed."

"Brownie?" Harmony asked. "Can I have it?"

"Ewww! Harmony!" Trin and I yelled together.

She shrugged. "Well, we are missing lunch today. I wish Candi were here. She could probably sneak us into the dining hall."

"No doubt. I guess everyone else is eating in town," Trin said.

I opened my suitcase. "Can we get by on this?"

"Mello, you're a lifesaver!" Harmony said, eyeing my baggie of chocolate pretzels mixed with peanuts. She sniffed the air. "But I vote we eat outside."

We invited Lamont to join our "picnic" and found a shaded bench.

"I'm glad we got the concert figured out," Trin said as we munched. "But I wish we had one more verse for that servant song."

"Sí," Harmony agreed. "I'll try to think of something. Tomorrow's going to be busy, though — we have to go to the beach to hand out flyers about the concert."

Lamont slapped his forehead with the palm of his hand. "Mr. Karuthers asked me to help design those," he said. "Mello, do you think you could find Candi? She probably knows where I can get onto a computer."

"Why does everything have to be about Candi?" I asked. "Since when is she everyone's hero? No, I can't find her, Lamont. Contrary to what all of you seem to think, we aren't linked by some secret-agent tracking system." *But we are linked*, I couldn't help thinking. *Or we were ...*

I stomped back to the cabin, grabbed a paper towel, and started scrubbing the floor.

chapter • 9

...

Friday Morning

I watched the campers ahead of me being herded onto buses like cattle heading in to be slaughtered. I turned to Harmony, Trin, and Lamont. "Don't you think we need one more practice?" I asked. "I'm still a little shaky on that servant song."

Harmony rolled her eyes. "Mello, we can't make you happy, can we? Yesterday you were mad about not handing out sandwiches to strangers."

"And today you don't want to hand out flyers about our own concert?" Trin added.

"That's the problem," I explained. "Doesn't it seem snotty to promote ourselves like that? Come see *me*. Come hear *me*. I'm so good, you don't want to miss *my* concert."

Lamont put a hand on my shoulder. "Yeah, that would sound snotty, if that's all the Chosen Girls were about. But is that really the point—for people to see *you*?"

"If it is, they'll be disappointed — no matter how hard we rock. We want to hook people up with God," Trin said. "As many as possible. So that's why we have to hand out these flyers." She tapped the stack of bright pink papers I held.

The line ahead of me moved up. Harmony gave me a little push from behind, and I started up the bus steps.

When we got to the beach, there were people everywhere.

"See?" Harmony asked. "It won't take five minutes to hand out twenty-five flyers."

"And as soon as our flyers are gone … free time!" Trin said. "Let's go."

I held my pink flyers and looked around. "But look," I said. "There are about a hundred other campers trying to get rid of their flyers too."

Lamont grabbed my elbow. "So don't just stand there. Be first. Be bold."

He dragged me toward a group of moms with little kids and whispered, "Ten people right there. Go for it." Then he disappeared.

I stepped forward and cleared my throat. No one looked at me. I moved closer and said, "Excuse me." One mom looked up and smiled — until she saw the papers in my hand.

"We're not interested," she snapped. She grabbed a little girl and pulled her closer, like I might try to kidnap her or something. I felt my face go hot. How could she think —

"It's just a concert tomorrow night on the — ," I began.

"I said no!" the woman interrupted.

I nodded and walked away.

I found a place between towels and blankets, where people passed on their way down the beach. I stood there, looking at each person who walked by. Surely someone would be curious. Someone might say, "May I have one of those papers? Oh, a concert? Wonderful!"

But no one did. People glanced at me and then quickly looked away. I looked down at my clothes. No embarrassing stains or anything. And I had on one of my favorite shirts. I wished I had a mirror. Maybe I had food between my teeth, or my hair had gone goofy. Or was it just me? Something about me made people want to get away as quickly as possible.

Maybe people didn't want my papers because they thought I was some kind of freak. That mom sure hadn't been impressed. She thought I wanted to take her kid.

"How many do you have left?" Harmony asked, walking up behind me.

I showed her the stack. "Twenty-five."

"What?" she asked. "Mello, you haven't given away *one*?"

Trin joined us. "I'm done," she announced. "That was way fun!"

"Sí!" Harmony agreed. "I met the nicest family from Oklahoma. They said they'll come. And so many cute guys! I love this beach."

Trin smiled. "Yeah. Everyone is so friendly. I even met a couple from Germany and some kids from Washington. So you still have some, Mello?"

I nodded.

"She has all twenty-five! She's done *nada*," Harmony said.

Trin looked shocked. "How? What have you been doing?" she asked.

"I've been right here," I explained. "No one wants them."

She tilted her head. "You aren't expecting people to ask for them, are you?"

I shrugged.

"Harmony, let's show her how it's done." Trin reached for my flyers, and I gave them to her. She handed half the stack to Harmony.

"Hello! Here's your free invitation to tomorrow night's big concert!" Trin said, shoving a flyer into the hand of the first guy to walk by.

"Cool. Thanks," he said, and kept walking.

"Free concert on the beach!" Harmony told a woman carrying a cooler.

The woman grabbed a flyer and looked at it. "Tomorrow night?" she asked.

"Sí! Right here," Harmony answered.

"Great!" the woman said before she walked away.

In five minutes, Trin and Harmony handed out my flyers. I stood by and watched them make about fifty new friends.

"It's only eleven. We've got tons of time," Trin said as the last paper left her hand. She pointed to a big clock on a lamppost. "Beach volleyball, here we come!"

"Beach volleyball?" I asked with a moan. "I'd rather hand out flyers."

Harmony led us to a game that had already started. The KCH guys and some Surf & Sand City campers had taken on a team of people I'd never seen before. It looked like their players must do nothing but hang at the beach and play volleyball. They could spike and dive and volley like professionals. Still, our team got it back over the net pretty well.

Cole saw us and called, "Yes! Reinforcements. Get in here and help us out. It's five to three, their favor."

"Did you already forget the Frisbee game?" I asked. "Are you sure you want us on your team?"

Hunter laughed. "Right now I don't care. I just want to rotate out."

Harmony and Trin lined up on the side of the court. Lamont went in for Hunter, who dropped onto the sand by us. "Are you psyched about the concert?" he asked.

"Yeah," Trin answered. "I hope we get a good crowd."

He looked around. "Out here? You will. People will be looking for something to do on a Saturday night, and you can't beat a free concert."

Lamont served and got it over the net. A tall, thin guy on the other team whacked it back across, and it hit the sand between two of our players. Everyone grumbled as they sent the ball to the other team for their serve.

Candi came up on the other side of the court. She watched and cheered but didn't come any closer to me. I wondered if she felt guilty because she had trashed our room.

Harmony rotated in, then Trin. They tried to get me in next.

"No thanks," I said, shaking my head. "I'm just a cheerleader today." I looked down the beach. Actually, this would be a great chance to take a walk. Be alone. Finally.

"Come on, Mello," Harmony called. "Just this once. Then you can say you've done it, and we'll leave you alone."

Trin held the ball out to me. "It's a game, Mello. Don't make a big deal out of it. It's just for fun."

I took the ball. "So if I don't think it's fun, does that mean I don't have to play?" I mumbled. I looked at all the people staring at me, waiting for the game to go on. I sighed, walked to the corner of the court, and stepped behind the line to serve.

I can't serve overhand, so I served underhand. To my complete surprise, the ball sailed over the net. Everyone cheered, and I felt relieved. When the other team returned the serve and Harmony hit it out of bounds, I got really happy. I didn't care that our team didn't get a point. I just didn't want to have to serve again, because I didn't think I'd get it over twice.

I made it okay through the next rotation. I tried to remember everything I'd learned in PE. Knees bent, arms straight, hands locked together. Watch the ball. Be ready. I actually did pretty well—especially since the ball never came to me.

That all changed after we rotated again. I took my place in the back left corner and assumed volleyball position. Harmony smiled back at me. "Muy bueno, Mello," she called.

I smiled. "Yeah, it's not too bad," I answered.

Cole served, and a guy on their front row jumped high, right at the net. He dinked it—just barely tapped it—and it landed at Trin's feet. Their team exploded into yells and cheers, and Trin rolled the ball to them.

"Sorry," Trin said, flashing us one of her movie star smiles.

"It's OK," Cole said.

"No big deal," Hunter added.

Harmony yelled, "Let's go, team. Stop them here! No points!"

I looked at the guy about to serve and said, "Right, Harmony."

He totally looked like an athlete. He lifted the ball with his left arm and barked, "Ten serving six." Then he brought his right hand behind the ball and stood frozen for a second. Every muscle in his arms and legs seemed carved or chiseled, like some famous Greek statue.

The next instant, I saw a flash of movement and heard a smack. *Thud.* The ball bounced off the sand in front of me.

"Huh?" I asked out loud. "Did he already hit it?"

Harmony laughed. "Sí. He's got a pretty good serve."

Trin said, "Don't worry, Mello. No one could have returned that ball."

"OK, team, be ready!" Karson called.

I looked at Statue-Man, already poised to spike again. "Eleven serving six."

Smack. Thud.

A cloud of sand rose to show where the ball hit and ricocheted off the court. Once again, right in front of me. Apparently, Statue-Man had some brains to go with his muscles. At least he had enough brains to see I made an easy target.

I glanced at the girl to my right. Taylor, built like a five-foot-eight toothpick and probably the only person from Surf & Sand City who was less athletic than me, played the center position. She shook her head. "Sorry, Mello," she said. "No way can I cover you. If by some miracle I got under the ball, that guy's serve would, like, break my arms."

"Twelve serving six."

Smack. Thud.

I got more and more embarrassed as each serve blasted my way.

"Thirteen serving six."

Smack. Thud.

"This is game point," Karson said. "We have to get it back over or they win."

"Thanks for the pressure," I answered.

"Fourteen serving six."

Smack.

I stepped forward, determined to get under the ball.

Thud.

Pain. Big, seeing-stars pain. Yeah, I got under the ball. It hit me right in the nose.

I couldn't stop the tears. My eyes turned into faucets twisted all the way on. That happens whenever I hurt my nose, and I always feel embarrassed. I try to explain that I'm not really crying; my eyes are just watering. But this time, the pain and the humiliation of the last six serves combined, and I *was* crying. Hard.

I put my hands to my face to see if my nose was still attached. It seemed to be.

Harmony put an arm around me and led me off the court. Trin made me sit down and started checking to see if my nose seemed broken. I half expected her to call 9-1-1.

Before they finished, Candi showed up with an ice pack. "Hold it on like this," she explained, slapping it onto my face.

I peeked over the ice pack at her and beyond to the circle of faces gathered around me. I felt like an exhibit at the state fair. Apparently, everyone from both teams had come to gawk. Even Statue-Man. When I looked at him, he said, "Sorry, dude."

"Thanks," I said. I looked back at Harmony. "I'll be fine. I'm just going to take a little walk, OK?"

"Sí," Harmony said. "Bueno idea. Everybody back off." She helped me up. "Where do you wanna go, amiga?"

"We could hit the ice-cream stand," Trin suggested.

"*We* aren't going anywhere," I answered. "I said *I am* going to take a walk, and that's what I meant. I haven't had five minutes alone since we left Hopetown."

I didn't give them a chance to answer. I didn't want to be talked into one more round of volleyball, or horseback riding, or boogie boarding. I wanted to walk, and I wanted to do it by myself.

So I left them behind and headed down the beach, alone.

chapter • 10

...

Friday Afternoon

I wished I had my book. I wanted to lose myself in a good story. Then I could forget about looking like an idiot during the volleyball game. And during Rollerblading. And after kayaking. And everything else I'd done at this stupid retreat.

This beach would totally be a nice, quiet place to read. Nothing as nice as my cliff at Surf & Sand City, but better than a bus full of noisy campers. I could finally get beyond the third paragraph.

But I didn't have my book. I remembered putting it in the bag with all my other stuff, but I'd left the bag on the bus. That fit in exactly with the way everything else had turned out since I got here.

I turned around to go get my stuff.

But to get to the bus, I'd have to walk back past the volleyball game. Everyone might gather around me again, poking my nose and apologizing.

Forget it.

I turned away and stomped along, holding the ice pack on my nose. I felt like every stranger on the beach stared at me. *Yes, I'm the weirdo with the flyers,* I thought. *The one who wanted to abduct your children. Someone finally decked me.*

I picked my way between beach towels and blankets and sun umbrellas. It irritated me that so many people had chosen to come to this particular beach on this particular day. California is a huge state with miles of coastline. Why couldn't all these people find somewhere else to bask in the sun?

I passed other volleyball games, and guys hanging out strumming guitars, and kids collecting seashells. After I'd walked for what felt like miles, the people finally started to thin out. The sandy beach ended, and I hit a stretch of big white rocks. I climbed along, carefully making my way from one to another. I fell once and re-scraped the strawberry on my left knee. I re-twisted my ankle on another rock, but just barely. At last I looked around and realized I'd accomplished it.

I was alone.

Or as alone as I could get on a public California beach. A few people tanned up the coast, a few swam down the coast, and an occasional hiker passed by. But it was good enough.

I sat down on a flat rock and faced the water. I drew my knees up under my chin and wrapped my arms around my legs. I transferred the ice pack from my nose to my ankle.

The waves crashed against the rocks below me, amazing me with their power. Droplets of water shot up and sparkled like hundreds of diamonds suspended in the air. A soft breeze lifted my hair, and I breathed deeply of the wet, salty air.

I traced the path of the sun on the water and noticed something moving out there. I squinted and caught my breath.

A school of dolphins! Their graceful black bodies reflected the sun as they arced through the air, jumping and twisting in a beautiful ballet. It looked like a Sea World show, but these dolphins weren't trained. They were wild and free, dancing for the joy of living. I felt goose bumps prickling my arms as I watched.

I tried to count. *One, two, three, four. Or was that the same one? No. Five, six. At least six. Wow.*

When they finally swam away, I felt exhilarated. I wished Harmony and Trin and Lamont could have seen them. But it had been my own private showing.

I closed my eyes to listen to the surf. The sound of waves had always been so peaceful and relaxing. But this time they made me think of the "Rhythm of the Sea" lessons I'd done with Candi. I heard her song—the sad song she had written about losing someone. My eyes flew open. I turned around. No, Candi wasn't there—I had only imagined it.

I closed my eyes again and thought of how she had shared her pain with me so openly. Why had I been so thoughtless? She didn't deserve to be hurt again—especially by someone she thought she could trust.

I wiped away a tear and tried to force myself to think of another song. I started humming the new tune Trin and Harmony came up with. Then I combined it with the words that had rolled around in the back of my mind since our last practice.

Too many obligations
all come with complications.
Can't find my inspiration.
I just really need a break.

Tell me what are the chances
to change the circumstances.
A hundred avalanches
are falling on me every day.

I tried to remember what our speaker at retreat talked about. Something about being a servant. I'd always thought that meant feeding the homeless and helping the less fortunate. But maybe there were other ways to serve.

If leading music in morning assembly was the way God wanted to work through me, I had blown it big-time. And if he'd brought Candi to me so I could help her through her grief, I'd blown that too.

But why? Why did I keep messing everything up?

What did that verse say? We'd studied it in every assembly. "Your attitude should be the same as that of Christ Jesus . . . who made himself nothing."

Had I made myself nothing? No. All week I had thought of one person: me.

Could it be that *I* needed an attitude adjustment?

"Can you help us? We want to build the biggest sand castle ever!" a little girl asked, stepping between me and the ocean. She flipped one of her two long pigtails behind her shoulder, stared at me from huge, hopeful green eyes, and said, "Please?"

I looked down the beach. I saw a group of kids digging and a mother looking around frantically. "Shelley!" the woman yelled. She looked our way.

Great. Another mom would think I wanted to abduct her kid.

She scrambled over rocks until she reached her daughter. She grabbed Shelley's elbow. "I'm so sorry!" she told me.

"She wanted to ask you to help, but I told her to leave you alone."

"But Mommy, she's lonely. See? She's been crying," the little girl insisted.

She turned to the girl. "Shelley, if you can't obey, we're going to have to go home. Please quit bothering this nice girl. I'm sure she doesn't want to build a castle, or she'd be doing it already."

Nice girl?

"Actually, I thought about building a castle, but I don't have a shovel," I said.

Shelley smiled. "You can use mine."

I looked at her mom. She smiled hopefully. "You would make her whole day," she said.

"I need to make someone's day," I answered, scrambling to my feet.

Shelley had two brothers and a sister. They all accepted me as one of the building crew, and we got busy.

I had forgotten how satisfying it is to pat damp sand into a bucket and turn it out, perfectly shaped and sparkling. I made the fat tower bases about a foot apart, and Shelley formed the walls connecting them with her hands. One brother made smaller towers on top of each of mine, and another found sticks to use for flags. Shelley's little sister decorated the whole thing with seashells.

"Why were you crying?" Shelley asked, taking a break from patting sand long enough to look into my eyes.

"Do you want the long version or the short version?" I asked.

Her older brother said, "The short version, please. We've got enough drama in our house with two girls."

I laughed. "Well, then, I hurt my ankle on one of those rocks," I explained.

We hadn't quite finished when Shelley's mom declared they had to leave. I wanted to whine along with the kids, but I tried to act mature. "Maybe I'll see you here again some day," I told Shelley, patting her on the head.

"Thank you for helping," she said. "It's the best castle we ever made."

"Yes, thanks," her mom echoed. "I actually got to read my book. That doesn't happen often."

I laughed. "Yeah, I can imagine." I added, "Hey, I'm in a band. We're doing a concert on this beach — down that way — tomorrow night. You should bring your family."

"Oh, Mom, can we?" Shelley's brothers asked.

"I think so," she answered. "And maybe we'll tell your cousins too." She explained, "They've got older cousins who live near here. They'd love a concert."

They gathered all their gear and headed away from the beach, with Shelley turning back to wave every few feet.

My stomach growled. I looked around and saw a snack stand ahead. I headed for it, suddenly starving. I could smell the hot dogs before I even saw the picture of one on the side of the stand, and my mouth started watering. I hoped they had plenty of mustard.

About ten feet from the stand, it hit me. I didn't have any money. It was in my bag on the bus. I watched people leaving the stand with huge cups of cold drinks, nachos, chips. I wanted something so badly, I almost went to the counter to beg. *Give me a hot dog and a drink. I'll come back to pay you, I promise.*

Nope. I had to get back to the bus. How far had I come?

I asked a couple leaving the stand what time it was. The man answered, "Three o'clock."

Three o'clock? I'd been wandering for hours! I couldn't miss the bus. What had Mr. Karuthers said? "This bus pulls out at four o'clock, with or without you. If you aren't on it, it's up to you to find a way back to Surf & Sand City." But my phone and my money were on the bus. I had to make it back.

chapter • 11

...

Friday Afternoon

I started jogging down the beach. My ankle ached, but before long that didn't matter because my side hurt worse.

My mouth went dry, and I thought I might pass out from dehydration. I hadn't even had a sip of water since we left Surf & Sand City. Breakfast felt like a lifetime ago.

The sun blazed down from a cloudless sky. If I didn't faint from hunger or thirst, heatstroke might get me. I could feel the skin on my face and shoulders burning. Of course my sunscreen was on the bus with everything else.

There were people everywhere, enjoying a holiday at the beach. Everyone looked relaxed and happy. All the people who had stared at me before didn't even glance my way now. No one cared that I might drop dead any minute or be left on this beach, alone and scared all night long.

I tried to get close to anyone who might be a camper. Surely I'd recognize someone from our retreat. But no. Every time I got close enough, the people were total strangers.

Where were Harmony and Trin? Why weren't they out looking for me? Didn't they even care? No. They were too busy doing exciting stuff and meeting new people.

I couldn't run anymore. I slowed to a walk. I had to force myself to take each step. What if I *did* faint? Would anyone from our group even notice if I didn't show up? Probably not. Who would miss a quiet spaz like me?

After the way I'd been acting, they might be glad to be rid of me.

I stopped and looked around. I didn't recognize a single thing about this part of the beach. Had I come too far? Had I already passed the place where the bus was parked? If so, I could walk for miles the wrong direction. Every step would take me farther from my friends and my ride back to Surf & Sand City.

I turned around and started back. No, that didn't seem right, either.

Too bad I didn't come equipped with a GPS.

I asked a lady in a huge straw hat for the time. "It's five till four," she said.

I walked away from her and whispered a prayer. *God, I need your help. In five minutes, the bus will leave. You know where it is. Won't you help me find it?*

I looked up and down the beach. Farther on, I thought I saw people playing sand volleyball.

Was that our court?

I ran all the way to it. Yes, it looked like the one we played on! No campers were there, though. They must all be on the bus.

I ran on, trying to remember where we had parked. Had five minutes already passed?

My heart skipped when I saw the place where I had first stumbled onto the beach, my stack of flyers in my hand. I turned away from the ocean and ran toward the parking lot, praying with each step. *Let the bus be there, God. Please let it still be there.*

It was. Only one of the many Surf & Sand City buses that had come to the beach was still there, but one was all I needed.

I ran to it and ran right up the steps.

"Finally!" someone yelled from the back of the bus. "We shoulda pulled out fifteen minutes ago."

"It's hot in here," another camper griped.

A blond guy said, "Yeah. Hope you had fun, 'cause we've been sitting here with nothing to do but sweat."

"Where did they find you?" skinny Taylor from the volleyball game asked.

I looked at her and said, "Where did who find me?"

"The other members of your band, Harmony and Trin," she answered.

"Yeah, where are they?" the bus driver asked, wiping sweat from his forehead.

I looked at him. "I didn't see them. I found the bus on my own."

"Oh, great!" half the bus moaned. "Now we have to wait for them."

The blond guy said, "Leave 'em. They know the rules. The bus leaves whether you're on it or not."

"That's not fair," Taylor complained. "They were on time — no, they were here early. When they didn't see Mello, they left to look for her." She pointed at me, and I wanted to disappear.

"I'll go find them," I told the driver.

"No you won't," he answered. "No one else leaves this bus."

"Hey, are we talking about the guitar players from morning assembly?" a brown-haired girl asked. She smacked her gum and looked at me.

"Yeah," I answered.

She said, "I saw them get in a big black van with some guys."

I shook my head. "No way."

"Yeah, I think they were skaters," she continued. "They were older. Scary-lookin' dudes."

I looked at the driver. "There is no way Harmony and Trin would get in a van with strangers."

"Unless they were forced," someone suggested.

The bus driver whipped out his phone. "OK. I'm calling the cops."

I dropped into the front seat and hid my face in my hands. I wanted to cover my ears, because the whole bus exploded into talk about Harmony and Trin.

"How scary!"

"Would they really be dumb enough to get in someone's van?"

"Maybe the guys didn't give them a choice."

"They could be in another state by now. The kidnappers could change the license plates and get lost in traffic."

"Did you see on the news, about the girl that got kidnapped last week?"

"Have they found her yet?"

"Nope."

"Wouldn't that be weird, to see Harmony's and Trin's pictures on the news?"

"And we'll say we were there when it happened."

"And tell how they were on the bus, ready to go, but they went back out to search for their friend."

"That's true sacrifice, man."

I tried to tune out the campers and listen to the bus driver talking to the police on his cell phone.

Cell phone!

I ran back to my old seat and found my bag. I dug out my phone and clicked on the picture of Harmony.

The theme song for *The Andy Griffith Show* filled the bus. I peeked over the seat back in front of me and wanted to cry. Harmony's and Trin's purses were both on the seat.

I dug in Harmony's and turned off her phone. Then I looked in Trin's bag. Yep. I found her phone too.

"Why didn't at least one of them take a phone?" I wailed.

Taylor sighed. "I don't think they thought it through. They said they'd already been out looking for you for a couple of hours. The bus was, like, their last hope. Then when you weren't here, they got pretty freaked out. They just took off."

Police sirens interrupted our conversation, and blue and red lights flickered through the bus windows.

At least four or five girls started crying.

I was too scared to cry.

Our driver said, "All right. Everybody remain calm." He pointed to the dark-haired girl who had seen the black van and then to me. "You come with me."

I swallowed hard and followed him down the steps.

The officers interviewed the other girl first. She smacked her gum the whole time she described the van and the men.

She acted like this was an exciting TV show and she was the star.

I kept thinking how scared my friends must be right now.

Next, the officers started asking me questions. What did Harmony and Trin look like? How old were they? Were they troublemakers?

"No," I answered, trying not to cry. "They never cause problems. It's my fault they weren't on the—"

"Mello!" Harmony yelled. She ran and threw her arms around me.

Trin came right behind her. "You're safe! Thank God!" She gaped at the police and the flashing lights. She put her hands on my shoulders (ouch!) and looked me up and down. "Are you OK? What's going on? Did someone try to hurt you?"

I laughed with relief. "The police are here for *you*," I explained. "How did you get away from those men?"

"What men?" Harmony asked.

"The skater dudes," I said. I pointed to the brown-haired girl. "She saw them force you into their van."

Trin shook her head. "No, we didn't get in any van."

We all looked at the brown-haired girl. She shrugged. "Guess I was wrong," she said. She looked at Trin and Harmony. "Come to think of it, the girls I saw didn't look much like you." She pointed at Trin. "I thought your hair was a lot shorter." She pointed at Harmony. "And I thought you had blonde hair."

"Blonde hair?" I asked, shocked. "Her hair is so black it's almost purple!"

She shrugged again, smacking away. "Sorry."

The police asked Harmony and Trin a few questions and said they were glad everything turned out well. Our driver told us to get on the bus and find our seats.

I wanted to apologize for being selfish all week … for everything. But by the time I dropped into the seat behind Trin and Harmony, everyone started pelting them with questions. How did they escape? Did they jump out of the van while it sped down the highway? Or had they wrestled the steering wheel away from the driver?

And what were the skaters like? Were they big? Old? Mean? Scary?

We made it halfway to Surf & Sand City before the people on the bus believed Trin and Harmony hadn't been abducted. Everyone seemed pretty disappointed with the truth. They had walked up and down the beach, looking for me. When they didn't find me after twenty minutes, they decided to come back for their phones. That's when they found me, surrounded by cops and flashing lights.

"So much for being on the news," someone in the back of the bus complained.

Trin said, "Yeah, well, sorry to let you down. We'll try to do something more exciting next time."

I leaned forward, sticking my head between Harmony and Trin. "Thanks for looking for me," I whispered. "I'm really glad you're OK."

They both turned and smiled at me. "Same," Trin said.

"Sí," Harmony agreed.

We pulled into the retreat center, and I sighed with relief. But now that the excitement and fear had worn off, I remembered how hungry and thirsty I felt. I almost ran to the dining hall.

I could apologize better after a cold drink and some food.

chapter • 12

...

Friday Evening

My stomach felt better after dinner, but everything else hurt. I went to the bathhouse to survey the damage.

I gasped when I saw my reflection in the mirror. My nose seemed bigger than I remembered, and it had a purplish-bluish tinge to it. Fortunately, the color didn't stand out much because the rest of my face had turned brilliantly red from sunburn.

I knew without looking that my scalp had been burned as badly as my face. That meant it would peel, and I'd find huge flakes of skin in my hair for days. Everyone would think I had mega-dandruff.

Tiny blisters covered my burned shoulders. I gingerly lifted the strap of my shirt and peeked under the material. The strip of white skin couldn't have been clearer if it had been painted on by a highway road crew.

I looked down at the scrape on my knee. A new scab had begun to form.

I tested my sore ankle. Yeah, it still hurt when I put weight on it.

I thought that was about it. I would survive.

Well, no more need to stall. After my shower, I would go to the cabin and do a thorough job of apologizing. I would start with my bad attitude before we left Hopetown and cover every stupid thing I'd done since. I felt better already just thinking about it.

But when I got to the cabin, Trin attacked me. "Look at this sunburn, Mello!" she yelled. She lay on her back on top of her sleeping bag, her arms crossed on her chest like an Egyptian mummy. Her skin tone matched her hot pink sleeping bag amazingly well. "My skin is on fire!" she griped.

"I know, I got burned today too," I answered. "It's miserable."

She shot an angry look my way. "Yeah, well, that wasn't *my* fault, was it?"

"Where were you, anyway?" Harmony asked. "We told everyone our side of the story, but we never heard where you went. Why couldn't we find you?"

Trin said, "She probably found some spa somewhere and got a massage."

"I did not!" I answered. "I helped a little kid named Shelley build a sand castle. And I invited her whole family to our concert."

"Right. That sounds just like something you'd do," Trin said sarcastically.

"Look," I shot back. "I didn't ask you to come look for me. I'm sorry you wasted your time and injured your precious skin, OK?"

I stalked out to the porch and sat down. I was mad at Trin for ruining my big apology and mad at myself for losing it again.

I waited until Trin and Harmony walked past me to go to the bathhouse. Then I went into the cabin, determined to go to sleep (or at least pretend to) before they got back.

I checked the alarm clock. Five thirty a.m.? No way. Not after a day like today. Yeah, we had to be at breakfast at seven thirty and assembly at eight thirty. But this once, Trin and Harmony would have to get by with less than two hours to primp. What on earth did they do for two hours, anyway? I knew what they did. They blasted fifty-decibel blow-dryers less than two feet from my head and talked and laughed together like I wasn't still in bed trying to sleep.

I set the clock for seven. Thirty minutes should be plenty of time.

I lay on top of my sleeping bag. When I felt the heat radiate from my skin, I discovered why Trin had adopted her mummy pose. My shoulders didn't hurt quite as bad when I crossed my arms that way. I tried to rearrange my legs, but they stuck to the leftover toothpaste. My nose throbbed with each beat of my heart.

It didn't look like it would be a very restful night.

I remembered the music video Lamont made for us when we first became a band and how it transformed us into superheroes.

Ha! I'm no superhero, I thought. *I can't even measure up as a regular person.*

I knew the superhero thing wasn't really about me, though. It was about God — his power, and how he works through us when we pray.

Prayer. Maybe I should try that.

•••

Saturday Morning

I must have slept eventually, because when I heard someone banging on our door, it took me a long time to figure out what the noise was and where it came from. It took even longer for me to realize I should respond in some way.

"Who is it? What do you want?" I yelled without even opening my eyes. My burning skin brought yesterday's disaster of getting lost on the beach back to me.

"It's Candi," she yelled through the door. "You missed breakfast. Assembly starts in ten minutes."

I opened my eyes. I could tell Harmony and Trin had also been sound asleep.

"What?" Trin screamed, sitting up on her bed.

Harmony crawled out of her sleeping bag and flew around the room. "Ten minutes? *No es bueno!* I'll have to take the fastest shower ever." She grabbed shampoo and soap.

"You can't take a shower," Trin corrected, picking up the alarm clock. "We barely have time to put clothes on. What happened? I had this thing set for five thirty."

I opened the door for Candi. She said, "When I didn't see you guys at breakfast, I got worried. I didn't want to bother you, but Lamont said I should make sure you were up."

"Thanks, Candi," I answered, running a brush through my hair. Ouch! Burned scalp. I pulled on a shirt and a skirt and slid into flip-flops. "Are you ready, Trin? Harmony?" I asked.

"Ready? I've only been conscious for thirty seconds!" Harmony complained. "Look at you, Mello. You look muy bonita. How do you do that in less than five minutes?"

I laughed. "My skin is bright red and my nose is purple. I don't think I look too glamorous. But the secret to getting ready fast in the morning is taking your shower the night before. I've been telling you that all week, but you won't listen."

"*You* turned off the alarm clock, didn't you?" Trin accused, stepping into cropped jeans.

I hoped my sunburn hid my flushing cheeks. "No, I didn't turn it off," I answered.

Harmony pushed her head through the neck of her T-shirt. She picked up the clock and looked at it from every angle, as if she expected to see fingerprints. "Did you reset it?" she asked me.

"Well … yeah," I admitted. "But I meant to set it for seven, so you'd still have time to get ready and eat breakfast."

"The little alarm light isn't on," Harmony announced. "You messed it up. And seven wouldn't have been early enough anyway."

"You don't have time to fight about it now," Candi pointed out. "The service starts in three minutes."

I helped Trin pull her pink hair into a loosely twisted knot, and Harmony pulled hers back with a couple of clips. We ran out the door and jogged to the auditorium. "We missed breakfast!" Harmony whined.

That did stink. I pushed on my growling stomach.

Mr. Karuthers shot us a seriously intense look as we slid into place onstage. He welcomed everyone, and we started playing. We didn't have a chance to tune, and it started off pretty ugly. We tuned as we went, but the music didn't get much better. We had to remind one another what songs came next. We looked sloppy and disorganized. No, we *were* sloppy and disorganized. I felt that familiar sense of embarrassment, and I couldn't wait to get off the stage.

After assembly ended and everyone left, they started in on me.

"So, did you enjoy sleeping in?" Trin asked.

Harmony huffed, "I hope so, because we sure paid for it. We totally bombed this morning—the last assembly of the week too."

"I can't believe I went onstage looking like this," Trin complained, patting her hair with her hands. "And I'm sure Mr. Karuthers felt disappointed. That was not worship—that thing we just did."

"I didn't mean to mess everything up. I just wanted a little more sleep," I began.

"And it's all about you, isn't it, Mello?" Harmony asked. "It has been all week. What you want to do, how you want to spend your time? What's best for Mello."

I put a hand up to stop her. "But—"

"But what? You want to be alone? That's what you've wanted all week, isn't it?" Trin asked. "Well, you've got it. Let's go, Harmony." She stomped toward the door.

"But—"

"I'm right behind you, Trin," Harmony answered as she followed. She looked back long enough to say, "This is your big day, Mello. The day your dreams come true. Enjoy it ... all alone."

The door banged shut.

Fine.

I started for the cabin to get my book. But I didn't want to read. I decided to find Candi.

I finally saw her sitting on the beach at Candi's Cove. I dropped down beside her and said, "Hey. How's it going?"

"OK, I guess," she answered, looking out over the ocean.

I didn't know where to start. "Thanks for waking us up this morning."

"Sure."

I listened to the kayaks knocking into one another every time a wave rolled through. "Um," I finally said, "did you know our room got trashed?"

"Yeah, sorry about that," she answered.

My heart sank, and I turned to her. "Why did you do it?" I asked.

"Do it? I didn't do it. I heard that Makayla chick bragging about it. Why would I trash your room?" She looked at me then — right into my eyes.

I looked away. "I thought you might be mad at me for what I said to Karson at the Sports Shack," I said. I held my breath.

She shook her head. "I don't know if mad is the right word. Sad, maybe. Or hurt. Or embarrassed that I thought you liked me when really —"

"Candi, wait," I interrupted. "I know that sounded bad — what I said to Karson. I don't even know why I said it like that." I looked at her and saw huge tears pouring out of her eyes.

"I get so nervous around him," I explained. "Everything I said was stupid — not just the stuff about you."

"You told me you were glad you spent the morning with me!" she said before she broke into sobs. Then she did that little hiccup thing. "I believed you, but you ... were ... lying!" She hunched over and buried her face in her arms.

Her shoulders shook, and I thought half the camp could probably hear her crying.

I patted her red curls. "No, Candi, I meant what I said to you. You're a great kid, and I like being your friend. Crud, you've been nicer to me than anyone else this week. Will you forgive me? Please?"

She kept her face buried a while longer. Then she finally looked up and blinked. "Yeah. OK, Mello." She smiled a sweet, watery smile that made me feel a hundred times worse.

"Thanks, girlfriend," I said. "I don't deserve you."

She said, "Yeah, but you're stuck with me!"

We talked for a while longer, and then I told her I needed to be alone. Not alone, really — I needed to spend some time with God.

•••

Saturday Afternoon

When Trin and Harmony came back to the cabin late in the afternoon, I was ready for them. I didn't give them a chance to start an argument or get me frustrated. They opened the door, and I said, "I've been a real twit all week, and I'm sorry."

"Ohwow," Trin joked, "we should put her in isolation more often!"

Harmony stared at me. "What? Where did this come from?" she asked.

I patted the bed on either side of me, and they came and sat down. Then Trin jumped up. "Ewww! I forgot about the toothpaste."

Harmony jumped up too, and they went to their own beds. "Go on," Harmony said.

"God's been working on me for a while," I told them. "All week, I guess. I didn't understand that verse in Philippians ... about being a servant. My attitude hasn't been the same as Jesus' attitude. I've been thinking of myself, just like Harmony said."

"I'm sorry," she interrupted. "I was way rude this morning."

"This is *my* apology," I said. "Let me be selfish this one last time, or I'll never get it out. I've been trying to say sorry to you both since yesterday, but you keep interrupting me."

"Oh!" Trin said. "I'm so sorry. Oops. I just did it again."

We all laughed.

"I didn't mean to be selfish," I explained. "I just wanted some peace and quiet. I'm not like you. I need to be alone sometimes." I wiped a tear off my cheek. "When things didn't turn out the way I planned, I fell apart. I forgot about the band, my friends, God ... everything but me. So ... I asked God for an attitude adjustment. And now I'm asking you to forgive me. Please?"

They jumped up and threw their arms around me.

"Ouch! Sunburn!" I reminded them.

"Me too. Ow," Trin said, backing away. She said, "Yeah, Mello, I forgive you. But will you forgive me for barging in on your retreat and making you do stuff you don't like to do?"

I stuck my hand out for a handshake. "Yeah."

"And me?" Harmony asked. "Do you forgive me for not seeing you were right?"

"Right about what?" I asked.

Harmony threw her hands out. "The whole time-alone thing. I thought the more we practiced, the better job we'd do leading music in assembly. But if we want people to worship God with us, we have to be ready to worship."

Trin nodded. "Maybe you can help us with that, Mello. Harmony and I love to be where the action is, but sometimes we need to be quiet and alone so we can hear what God is telling us."

I smiled. "That reminds me. You're going to love what I've done with that song you wrote. I know the concert's in, like, a couple of hours, but I want to sing my version for you. If you like it, maybe we could sing it that way tonight."

"Sure," Trin said.

Harmony agreed. "Sounds good."

"So . . . first, this seems like a good time to pray," I offered.

We held hands, and I started to pray. "God, I'm sorry I've been so selfish. Give me a new attitude. Let me be a servant who puts others first."

"God, I've been so busy having fun, I haven't stopped to listen to you this week," Harmony prayed. "Forgive me for trying to show others how to worship, when I wasn't ready myself."

Trin said, "God, we love you. Thanks for choosing us to be your servants, to be friends with each other, and to be in this band. Thanks for the way-fabulous opportunity we have at tonight's concert. Use us, God. Speak through our music and through our lives. Amen."

• • •

Saturday Evening

The concrete stage stood eight feet off the ground, with three plain white walls set at angles to form a backdrop.

Nothing fancy about it, but then, there didn't need to be. It stood on a sandy, palm-lined beach, with the Pacific Ocean putting on its own show less than a hundred feet away.

I did a few drills on snare. "I'm glad the stage is sideways to the beach, so we can see the water too," I said. "This is going to be awesome."

Harmony finished tuning. "Sí. Muy bueno."

"I'm glad KCH agreed to open for us," Trin added. "This could have been their deal, you know?"

"Do you wish it was, Mello? That we'd never agreed to do the concert?" Harmony asked.

I tapped the cymbal. "No way. We're right where we're supposed to be."

"No," Lamont corrected, climbing the stairs onto the stage. "Actually, you're supposed to be backstage. KCH is ready to come out."

I looked over the crowd before I headed back. The Surf & Sand City campers seemed to fill the beach, but I could see other people too. I saw Shelley and her family and waved to them. Anna and Emily smiled at me. And Candi flashed me a thumbs-up.

"Let's sit back there and just watch the sun go down," Trin said, tugging my sleeve.

"And listen to the waves," Harmony added. She smiled at me. "A few quiet minutes before the whole beach explodes with music."

KCH rocked. By the time Mr. Karuthers announced us, the crowd had tripled. I couldn't even see where the people ended.

We opened with "The Girl I Wanna Be" and then sang "You've Chosen Me." Everything went well until "Love

Lessons." By the end of that song, my palms were so sweaty, I could hardly hold my sticks. I couldn't believe what I'd decided to do next. Not even Trin or Harmony knew about it. If only I hadn't told Lamont, I could still back out.

The song ended, and I rushed backstage with Harmony. We quickly ripped off the clothes we had on over our super suits. Or we tried to be quick. I felt so nervous, I could hardly undo the buttons on my shirt.

"Listen. Trin's doing great," Harmony whispered.

I listened. Trin said, "You might have noticed our songs are a little different. Every band writes songs that come out of their own experience. Our experience — as a band and as individuals — has been wrapped up in a power bigger than ourselves. We've found we just can't do anything right without God's help. So most of our songs are prayers asking him to help us. Asking him to change us."

"Wow! I should have left it up to Trin. She sounds good. I'm scared about talking," Harmony admitted. "Can you believe that? All I do is talk. But man, there must be a couple thousand people out there! Did you see them all?"

"Don't remind me," I wailed. "I might run away instead of finishing the concert."

Harmony grabbed my arm and pulled me back onstage as Trin finished speaking. Harmony went straight to the place Lamont had marked with a piece of masking tape. He turned the light so it shone on her face — perfect.

Harmony smiled and started to speak, and I'm sure not a soul there could have guessed she felt nervous. "Our band is called the Chosen Girls because we're excited that God chose us. He proved it by sending Jesus to die for our sins. And not just ours — God chose you too. He loves you. He wants you to belong to him. When you do, the Bible says you're a new creation. He can do amazing things through ordinary people when we let him work through us. Through him, anything is possible."

I stood, listening, on the place Lamont had marked for me. I concentrated hard on not throwing up. *What if he turns that light on my face, and at that exact instant I start barfing? No! Don't think about vomit. Think about what you're going to say. Which is . . . what? What's the first word? I can't remember the first word!*

The light shone in my eyes. My turn! My head pounded and my legs felt all weak, but I made myself speak. "Sometimes when you pray, God does amazing things through you — like Harmony said. But other times he does amazing things *in you*. The last song we're going to sing tonight came from something God did in my life this week.

"I thought doing the right thing is all that matters, but it's not. If you do the right thing for the wrong reason, or with a bad attitude, it's not the right thing anymore." I tried to look into the audience, but the glare of the spotlight blinded me. "I've been totally selfish, but I've asked God — and my friends — to forgive me. And they have. It feels so great to be forgiven. And I'm glad God doesn't just forgive — he changes hearts. I thank him for changing mine this week.

"God also led me to someone special, who helped me realize it's OK to talk about your deepest hurts, as long as the person you're talking to is a true friend. Is my true friend Candi still out there?" I asked.

She answered with a *whoop*.

"Come up onstage, Candi," I called. "We need your help on this song. Please, everyone, give it up for Candi!"

In less than a minute, she stood beside me. I reached behind a monitor and pulled out her little drum. I handed it to her and whispered. "Just play the backbeat. You can do it!"

Lamont cut the light, and I ran to my drum set. When the stage lights came back on, with swirling colors dancing, the crowd roared its approval. Even Candi looked surprised by our super suits. We had pulled it off.

Harmony and Trin smiled at me as I started the beat for our new song, "Time." Actually, I'm not sure *smiled* is the right word. *Gaped in astonishment* is more like it. They looked even more surprised than I felt that I had managed to talk in front of that many people.

Too many obligations
all come with complications.
Can't find my inspiration.
I just really need a break.
When I'm down to nothing,
downtime fills me up and
I can give back something
more than I came in with.
Your word guides my spirit.
Help me, Lord, to hear it.

I played and sang my heart out. I looked at the yellows and oranges of the sun going down over the water on my left, the beauty of the swaying palms on my right, and the hundreds — maybe thousands — of people in front of me.

We sang the chorus:

I just need some me time — free time.
Time to hang out with nothin' to prove
Gotta have some downtime — found time.

Kickin' it around time
to open my heart to the truth.
Time to be clearer.
Time to be nearer to you.

I watched Candi beat her drum for all she was worth—hitting perfectly on beats two and four. Her face glowed, and her smile made her beautiful.

I thought about the crazy ways I had tried to get away during the week: The spa trip that made my best friends mad. The escape on the beach that got the police involved. The alarm-clock fiasco that upset Mr. Karuthers. All attempts to get away from people and noise and find some calm and quiet.

But there, during the closing song, the craziest thing happened. In the middle of the blaring music, surrounded by thousands of people, I realized I was right where God wanted me.

And then it happened. I finally found peace.

BIG BREAK

Created & Illustrated by G Studios
Written by Cheryl Crouch

chapter • 1

...

Thursday

Yesterday I stopped for a slushy at the Quik Shop. I was standing there watching it ooze into my cup when someone said, "Can I get my picture made with you?" I didn't realize she might be talking to me. "Please?" the voice asked.

I turned around, and a young girl smiled up at me and showed me her camera. She asked, "Aren't you Harmony from the Chosen Girls?"

I asked her name and stuff — like people always want my photo. Then I felt something cold and sticky on my hand. The frozen cherry cola had overflowed my cup and was glopping into the little drain underneath it.

That's what I get for trying to act cool. I licked the stuff off my hand and followed her to the counter, where the clerk snapped our picture.

Isn't that amazing? I mean, just when I'm doing something totally normal, I get reminded that I'm — well, kind of a rock star. Don't think I'm complaining. Oh, no. The fame thing is muy bueno.

But I get this feeling there's more to it, that our band hasn't made it big just so people will recognize me at the Quik Shop. Like maybe I'm famous for a reason —

. . .

Thursday Afternoon

Trin burst into my room. "Harmony! Are you psyched or what?"

I jumped up and screamed, "I know! Only two days until . . ." Then we both yelled, "Hopetown Battle of the Bands!" Trin broke into a dance and I did an air guitar solo and sang, "I can't wait to play my bass. Onstage, that's my favorite place. Oh, yeah!"

"You're crazy — both of you." My forever best friend, Mello, sat in her spot between throw pillows at the head of my bed.

My new best friend, Trin, tossed a plastic bag onto Mello's lap. "You're so right," she agreed. "That's why we need you, Mello. You keep us grounded." Trin watched Mello pull a pair of white pants out of the bag. "Plus you can sew," she added, tossing us one of her stunning movie star smiles as she flounced across to my sister Julia's bed.

"What did you do this time?" Mello asked, inspecting the torn hem.

"My boots caught on them at our last concert," Trin answered. "Sorry. Can you fix it?"

Mello rolled her eyes. "You don't pay me enough for this, you know," she complained.

Trin looked shocked. "You get paid?"

Mello sighed. "Do you have a needle and thread, Harmony?"

"Somewhere," I answered, digging through my dresser drawers. I pulled out old hair clips, two markers, a rubber band, and some tape. "Just give me a minute." I added some smiley-face stickers and two candy wrappers to the pile.

Mello laughed. "What a mess. How can you find anything, Harmony? I should just go home and get my sewing kit. Save some time."

"Ouch!" I yelped, yanking my hand out of the drawer. "See?" I reached back in carefully and held up my prize. "You should have more faith in me. I found a needle."

"Thanks. Sorry you had to spill your blood for it. And how's *your* super suit?" she asked me, taking the needle from my hand. "I might as well solve everyone's problems at the same time."

"Mine's OK, I think," I said, digging for thread. "Ta-da! Look at this. It's even white. I'm organized in my own scary way." I handed the spool to Mello and crossed the room to my closet. I reached in and grabbed the white suit with the huge cross sewn on the front. I laid it on the end of my bed and looked it over. "Mine's fine. You did a great job on these, Mello. You're an amazing seamstress, or whatever it's called."

Mello blushed and stared hard at the needle as she poked it through the white pants. "Thanks. But all I did was put them together. You designed them."

"That was easy," I said. "I just tried to make them look like the ones in Lamont's music video." I stood there staring at the outfit, remembering the first time we watched the *You've Chosen Me* DVD. Mello's next-door neighbor Lamont had turned the three of us into superheroes, defeating evil monsters through special effects he created to help us enter a music video contest.

"Hello?" Trin asked. "Harmony, you're totally zoned out. What are you thinking about?"

"My super suit. How cool it would be if it wasn't just a costume."

Mello groaned. "It's *not* just a costume. It's a symbol."

"It stands for God's power working through us," Trin added.

"I know, I know," I answered. "But don't you ever want to see it happen? In real life? You know, right versus wrong. Change the world. That kind of stuff."

"I do see it, Harmony," Mello insisted. "It's in our music — that's how we're changing the world."

I carried my outfit back to the closet and slipped the hanger onto the rod. I smoothed out the suit, then stepped back and closed the door. "I guess so," I agreed. "And Friday's a big day for that, huh? Loads of people will be there."

"I'm scared out of my mind about this Battle of the Bands," Mello admitted. "Why are you so psyched about it?"

"Like you said — that's how we're changing the world," I answered. "At least for now."

• • •

Thursday

For Thursday's practice, I decided to surprise everyone by bringing our number one official snack: chocolate-covered pretzels mixed with peanuts. At the grocery store I grabbed the stuff and looked for the shortest line.

I found an express lane with only one woman checking out. Well, one woman, her two little kids, and a baby. I got in line behind them and smiled at the tiny girls who peeked at me from behind their mom. One of them turned away, but the chubby one smiled back without taking her thumb out of her mouth.

The mom had a hard time getting money out of the diaper bag because she was holding the baby. She moved him to her other arm and put the bag on the counter, digging through it with her right hand.

"I know there's more in here somewhere," she said, pausing to tuck a strand of long brown hair behind her ear. She pulled out wipes, a pacifier, and a stuffed animal. She turned her enormous blue eyes to me. "I'm sorry this is taking so long. I guess I shouldn't be in the express lane ..."

I told her it was fine, even though I did feel a little irritated. Because of her, I'd be late for practice at the shed. Couldn't she keep all her money in the outside pocket? How hard is that?

She started putting stuff back in her bag and said, "Um ... I won't get the bananas. Or the grapes. Sorry—"

The girl with her thumb in her mouth said, "'Nanas!"

Her mom said, "Maybe next time, sweetie."

The little girl whimpered. "I want 'nanas. *Pweese*, Mommy."

I looked at the other stuff moving down the conveyor belt toward the bags. Diapers, milk, eggs. Then I looked at the mom, whose eyes started to water and redden. "I said we'll try next time," she whispered to her daughter.

Oh. I finally got it. It wasn't that she couldn't *find* the money. She didn't *have* the money. For bananas and grapes.

The checker guy set the fruit aside, and the woman paid for everything else. She moved her kids to the end of the counter and started putting stuff in bags.

I looked at the family, but suddenly I saw myself with Mamma and my sister and brother ten years ago. We'd just moved to the States from Peru, and my papi couldn't find work. The money they brought to live on was gone.

I had asked Mamma for bananas. "Yo quiero plátanos. Por favor, Mamma."

"Luego, mia mija," Mamma answered.

I felt the tears streaming down my face as I blinked away this vision of my own hungry childhood.

"Eight forty-two," the checker said in a loud voice. I blinked again and looked at him. He seemed irritated.

I whispered, "I'll take the bananas and grapes, please."

He shrugged and rang them up with my snack stuff.

I grabbed it all and ran to catch the mom. "Excuse me," I said, tugging on her sleeve.

She turned around. I said, "Um, I got those bananas. And the grapes — for your kids."

She stood up real tall and stuck her nose in the air. I could tell she wanted to say no.

I didn't give her a chance. "I know how it is — I'm kinda organizationally challenged too," I said with a laugh. "I've done that before, where I can't find my money. Please take it." I held the bag out. The little thumb-sucker reached for it. Her mom pulled her away.

"Maybe I'll see you in here again," I continued. "Then you can pay me back. After you find your money."

I watched the mom's blue eyes get all watery again, but this time she smiled. "Thanks," she said. "I'll look for you."

I practically ran to the garage in Mello's backyard where we used to play dolls and house when we were little. Now it's our studio — and a way cool place to hang. We call it the shed.

They were already warming up when I threw the door open. "I know what we can do!" I shouted.

Mello's drumsticks froze, and Trin's last guitar note hung in the air. Lamont looked up from the soundboard.

"We can feed hungry kids," I said. "Let's start a food pantry right here in Hopetown."

"And this idea came from ... where?" Trin asked.

"Does it matter?" I shot back. "There are kids in our town who can't eat decent food because their parents don't have enough money. *We* have money for fun stuff like, like ... chocolate-covered pretzels and peanuts." I held the bag up. "And we should help."

Trin put her guitar down and reached for the bag. I handed it to her. "So, are you in?" I asked.

"Starting a food pantry is a big deal," Mello said, grabbing an empty bowl and holding it out as Trin dumped out the pretzels and peanuts.

"Seriously," Lamont added. "You have to have a building and workers and ... food." He stuffed his mouth full and started chewing.

"We can get all that," I insisted.

Lamont flopped onto the old tan couch. "How?"

"With the money from Chosen Girls."

Mello shook her head. "It's not like we have unlimited funds, Harmony. If we start a food pantry, people need to be able to count on it. What if people got used to coming, and then we ran out of money and had to shut it down?"

"We'll just have to make sure that doesn't happen," I answered.

Trin said, "And your plan for doing that is … ?"

My phone rang the tune for Unknown.

I answered it, and a woman started talking so fast my brain could hardly keep up.

"This is Larinda Higgins. I'm a talent agent with the Shining Stars Agency out of New York City. I'm sure you've heard of us—we represent many of the biggest names in pop, rock, and country music today. I am speaking with Harmony Gomez, correct? And you are the manager for the Chosen Girls?"

I gulped but finally managed to say yes.

"Good!" she said. "I know a bright, talented, young band manager like yourself would of course be busy looking out for the best interests of your band. I'm sure you've spent hours researching talent agencies—"

"Well, actually—"

"No doubt that's how you know about Shining Stars. Maybe you were afraid to call a company as large and well-known as ours, Harmony. I can certainly understand why. The Chosen Girls are untried, really. A few concerts under your belts, a few contests, yes, but, frankly, nothing like the big names our company usually represents."

"Um, uh, OK …," I stammered.

"Don't be offended, Harmony. Everyone has to start some-where. It's amazing you've accomplished what you have without an agent. It's a dog-eat-dog world out there. I'm sure you've discovered that by now. Am I right?"

I tried to think. "Well, yeah, I guess …"

"That's why I am thrilled to be the one to tell you this unbelievable news. Harmony, the Shining Stars Agency is interested in the Chosen Girls!"

My heart beat faster.

"I'm not prepared to offer you a contract, you understand," she continued. "But we have our eye on you. In fact, I will be at tomorrow's Battle of the Bands myself, to watch the Chosen Girls perform. Who knows? If I like what I see tomorrow, well, let's just say the sky is the limit for your little band."

The line went dead.

"Who was that?" Trin asked.

I jumped up and down and screamed. "That, *mis amigas*, was the answer we've been looking for. The hungry children of Hopetown can count on us — as long as we win the Battle of the Bands tomorrow."

zonderkidz

Chosen Girls is a dynamic new series that communicates a message of empowerment and hope to Christian youth who want to live out their faith. These courageous and compelling girls stand for their beliefs and encourage others to do the same. When their cross-cultural outreach band takes off, Trinity, Melody, and Harmony explode onto the scene with style, hot music, and genuine, age-relatable content.

Backstage Pass

Book One • Softcover • ISBN 0-310-71267-X

In *Backstage Pass*, shy, reserved Melody gets her world rocked when a new girl moves in across the street from her best friend, Harmony. Soon downtime—or any time with Harmony at all—looks like a thing of the past as the strong-willed Trinity invades Melody and Harmony's world and insists that the three start a rock band.

Available now at your local bookstore!

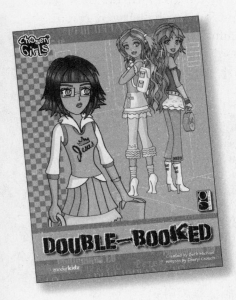

Double-Booked

Book Two • Softcover • ISBN 0-310-71268-8

In *Double-Booked*, Harmony finds that a three-way friendship is challenging, with Trinity befriending a snobby clique and Melody all negative. Through a series of mistakes, Harmony unwittingly unites the two against her and learns that innocent comments hurt more than you think. Ultimately, the Chosen Girls are united again in time to sing for a crowd that really needs to hear what they have to say.

Unplugged

Book Three • Softcover • ISBN 0-310-71269-6

The band lands a fantastic opportunity to travel to Russia, but the "international tour," as they dub it, brings out Trinity's take-charge personality. Almost too confidently, she tries to control fundraising efforts and the tour to avoid another mess by Harmony. But cultural challenges, band member clashes, and some messes of her own convince Trinity she's not really in charge after all. God is. And his plan includes changed lives, deepened faith, and improved relationships with her mom and friends.

zonderkidz

zonder**kidz**

Big Break

Book Five • Softcover • ISBN 0-310-71271-8

The Chosen Girls are back! As opportunities for the band continue to grow, Harmony can't resist what she sees as a big break ... and what could be better than getting signed by an agent?

Sold Out

Book Six • Softcover • ISBN 0-310-71272-6

Dedicated to proving herself to others, Trinity gets involved in organizing the school talent show. Before she knows it, she accepts a dare from Chosen Girls' rival band to be decided by the outcome of a commercial audition.

Available November 2007 at your local bookstore!

Overload

Book Seven • Softcover • ISBN 0-310-71273-4

Melody discovers a latent talent for leadership that she never knew she had. When she begins a grief recovery group for kids like her, she loses her focus on the work God is doing through the Chosen Girls.

Reality Tour

Book Eight • Softcover • ISBN 0-310-71274-2

When the Chosen Girls go on their first multi-city tour in a borrowed RV, Harmony's messiness almost spoils their final show. What's worse, she almost blows her opportunity to witness to her cousin Lucinda.

zonder**kidz**

zonder**kidz**.

We want to hear from you. Please send your comments
about this book to us in care of zreview@zondervan.com. Thank you.

Grand Rapids, MI 49530
www.zonderkidz.com

ZONDERVAN.com/
AUTHORTRACKER
follow your favorite authors